You're About to Become a

Privileged Woman.

INTRODUCING
PAGES & PRIVILEGES™.

It's our way of thanking you for buying
our books at your favorite retail store.

— *GET ALL THIS FREE* —
WITH JUST ONE PROOF OF PURCHASE:

◆ **Hotel Discounts** up
to 60% at home and
abroad ◆ **Travel Service**
- Guaranteed lowest
published airfares
plus 5% cash back

**$50
VALUE**

on tickets ◆ **$25 Travel Voucher**

◆ **Sensuous Petite Parfumerie** collection

◆ **Insider Tips Letter**
with sneak previews
of upcoming books

*You'll get a FREE personal card, too.
It's your passport to all these benefits– and to
even more great gifts & benefits to come!*

There's no club to join. No purchase commitment. No obligation.

Enrollment Form

☐ *Yes!* I WANT TO BE A *P*RIVILEGED *W*OMAN.

Enclosed is one *PAGES & PRIVILEGES*™ Proof of Purchase from any Harlequin or Silhouette book currently for sale in stores (Proofs of Purchase are found on the back pages of books) and the store cash register receipt. Please enroll me in *PAGES & PRIVILEGES*™. Send my Welcome Kit and FREE Gifts -- and activate my FREE benefits -- immediately.

More great gifts and benefits to come like these luxurious Truly Lace and L'Effleur gift baskets.

NAME (please print)
_____

ADDRESS _____ APT. NO _____

CITY _____ STATE _____ ZIP/POSTAL CODE _____

PROOF OF PURCHASE

Please allow 6-8 weeks for delivery. Quantities are limited. We reserve the right to substitute items. Enroll before October 31, 1995 and receive one full year of benefits.

NO CLUB!
NO COMMITMENT!
Just one purchase brings you great **Free Gifts** and **Benefits!**
(More details in back of this book.)

Name of store where this book was purchased_____

Date of purchase_____

Type of store:

☐ Bookstore ☐ Supermarket ☐ Drugstore

☐ Dept. or discount store (e.g. K-Mart or Walmart)

☐ Other (specify)_____

Which Harlequin or Silhouette series do you usually read? _____

Complete and mail with one Proof of Purchase and store receipt to:

U.S.: *PAGES & PRIVILEGES*™, P.O. Box 1960, Danbury, CT 06813-1960

Canada: *PAGES & PRIVILEGES*™, 49-6A The Donway West, P.O. 813, North York, ON M3C 2E8   PRINTED IN U.S.A

Despite Clare's past,
Fen Marchand agreed
to try her out as
his housekeeper.

Almost immediately, there was an intense physical attraction between them, but Clare's experiences had taught her to keep her distance. She just couldn't tell Fen the truth about why she'd done what she'd done—because he would never understand....

ALISON FRASER was born and brought up in the far north of Scotland. She studied English literature at university and taught math for a while. Then she became a computer programmer. She took up writing as a hobby and it is still very much so, in that she doesn't take it too seriously! Alison has two dogs, three children, but only one husband. Currently she lives in West Yorkshire, England, and is in her late thirties—but she doesn't yet know what she'd like to be when she grows up!

Books by Alison Fraser

HARLEQUIN PRESENTS
1425—TIME TO LET GO
1675—LOVE WITHOUT REASON

ALISON FRASER

Tainted Love

Harlequin Books

TORONTO • NEW YORK • LONDON
AMSTERDAM • PARIS • SYDNEY • HAMBURG
STOCKHOLM • ATHENS • TOKYO • MILAN
MADRID • WARSAW • BUDAPEST • AUCKLAND

ISBN 0-373-11753-1

TAINTED LOVE

Copyright © 1994 by Alison Fraser.

First North American Publication 1995.

Printed in U.S.A.

CHAPTER ONE

IT WAS summer when Clare was released, but it might as well have been winter. The sun did not touch her. Nothing did. They'd called her cold-hearted and she'd become so.

The day of her job interview was especially hot. In Oxford, summer students paraded tanned limbs in white T-shirts and shorts. Clare wore black. Black jacket. Black skirt. Black court shoes. The only relief was a cream-coloured blouse. She'd aimed for respectability and succeeded to the point of drabness. She didn't care.

Need alone had prompted her to go for the job. Her prison visitor, Louise Carlton, had a brother who needed a housekeeper. She believed Clare might suit the post. Clare didn't. She didn't think the brother would either, but Louise had badgered her into an interview.

She walked from the rail to the bus station, caught the two o'clock to Chipping Haycastle and got off at the Old Corn Mill as instructed. She walked for perhaps quarter of a mile, before she reached two iron gates set in a six-foot-high wall. 'Woodside Hall' was etched into the stone.

She peered beyond and saw only a tangle of woodland through which a tarred drive disappeared. She pushed at the gates. She'd been told they would be open. They weren't. There was no chain on them and she wondered if they were electronically operated. She pushed again and they gave a little. She looked downwards to discover they'd been tied shut with string.

She bent down to untie the string and heard a sound. She glanced round her but saw no one. She started to unpick the string and heard the sound again. This time there was no doubt. It was the sound of a child's laughter and she caught a glimpse of a head bobbing up from a clump of shrub on the far side of the gates.

'Hello,' she called out to tell the child he'd been spotted.

There was no response, just the rustling of bushes as the hidden figure made a getaway.

That, she assumed, would be Master Miles Marchand. A sweet boy according to his aunt Louise. Clare wondered if tying the gates together came under the category of 'sweet'.

The string had been knotted many times and it took her about ten minutes to untie it. The next hurdle was waiting for her round a bend in the drive. She could hardly miss it—a piece of twine, a foot off the ground, running from a tree on one side of the road to a tree on the other. Presumably she was meant to trip up on it and take a flier.

Instead she stepped over it and called out, 'Sorry. Too obvious, I'm afraid.'

This time there was no response, not even a rustle of leaves, but she was still sure he was watching her. She sensed it as she went up the winding drive to the house.

It was an early Georgian manor house of considerable size: six windows wide and three storeys high. She knew Louise was wealthy. It seemed her brother was, too.

She passed a Jaguar and a Mercedes saloon, and went up to the huge oak door. She pulled the bell at one side, and waited. And waited. And waited. Assuming it hadn't been heard, she rang it again. By her third attempt, she decided it couldn't be working.

She lifted the lion's-head knocker on the door, and it came away in her hand. She was left wondering how the heavy lead object could possibly have unscrewed itself from the door. Then she heard the sound of childish laughter again.

It was clear that one member of the household definitely didn't want a new housekeeper, and she wasn't sure if she wanted to volunteer for the post, either. It wasn't as if she knew much about children. Just Peter, and that had been a long time ago—so long she could almost think of him without pain.

She felt this other boy's eyes on her as she circled the house, searching for signs of life. She heard the drift of voices coming from an open French window, and came closer. She recognised Louise's as the female voice. The other she assumed belonged to Fenwick Marchand, the eccentrically named master of the house.

Clare approached the doorway, intending to announce her presence, but got as far as lifting her hand to knock before the man's voice arrested her on the spot.

'Honestly, Lou, you don't really expect me to give this woman a job,' he declared. 'Charity's one thing. Ask me for a donation—fine, you'll get one. But if you think I'm going to open up my home to some...some...whatever the hell she is.'

'She's a very nice girl who's had a rough time of it,' Louise Carlton replied in a soft, kindly tone that contrasted sharply with her brother's. 'If you knew what has happened to her——'

'Well, I don't, do I?' Marchand jumped in again. 'Because you refuse to tell me.'

'Only because you'd get the wrong idea, Fen,' his sister went on calmly, 'and what she was convicted of is irrelevant.'

'To you, maybe,' the man countered. 'But then you aren't about to share your home with some thief or drug addict or murderer. Possibly all three, for all I know.'

'I've told you. She was innocent,' Louise said with utter conviction.

It drew a scoff of laughter in response.

Clare pursed her lips. She couldn't see Marchand, because he was seated in a high armchair. But she saw Louise Carlton, standing before him, looking upset and flustered as she tried to appeal to her brother's better nature.

Clare could have told her not to bother. The owner of that deep, sarcastic voice had no better side, and Clare felt no compunction about eavesdropping.

'Clare has never discussed her case with me,' Louise Carlton claimed in perfect truth. 'She has never asked anything of me, either. I was the one who suggested this post to her, knowing she needs work and you need a housekeeper.'

'Need, yes,' he agreed, 'am desperate for, no. And I'd have to be to employ this woman. I ask you, do you really want Miles exposed to her influence?'

'He could do worse,' Louise said, on the defensive.

'He already has done,' Fenwick reminded her. 'I don't think I fancy him adding lock-picking or safe-cracking to his list of other doubtful interests.'

This time Louise didn't respond, but her face gave her away, colouring slightly at the reference to safe-cracking.

Her brother was quick to spot it. 'So that's what she is—a professional thief.'

'No, don't be ridiculous,' Louise dismissed the idea hastily, before ruining Clare's chances with the admission, 'Stealing may have been one of the things she was accused of, but——'

'*One* of the things?' Fenwick's voice rose in disbelief. 'How many *more* are there?'

Louise shook her head. 'I told you. It doesn't matter. You have my word she's a reformed character.'

'Really?' His voice became a sarcastic drawl. 'I thought you said she was innocent.'

'She is.'

'Then she wouldn't need to be reformed, would she?'

'I...' Louise Carlton frowned over her brother's logic. 'Stop trying to confuse me, Fen. We both know you're cleverer with words—and pretty much everything else. But I do know people better than you.'

'Possibly,' he conceded. 'At any rate, you saw through that bitch I married.'

'*Fen*!' his sister reproved in shocked tones.

'What? I mustn't call her a bitch, because she's dead,' he scoffed. 'Is that it?'

'Well, yes...' Louise admitted that that was what she meant.

'I called her such long before she drove off a cliff with her toy-boy lover,' he pointed out. 'I don't see why she should be canonised now she's dead.'

'Maybe not,' his sister agreed, 'but you have to be careful. It wouldn't be very nice if Miles overheard you.'

'Miles isn't likely to,' he dismissed. 'Having discovered there was another candidate for housekeeper, he took himself off to his hut in the woods and is no doubt scheming on how to get rid of the lady, should I be rash enough to employ her.'

'You told him about Clare?' Louise said in exasperation.

'That she was coming, yes,' her brother confirmed, 'that she was an arch-villain, no. If I had, knowing Miles, he would probably have wanted me to hire her.'

'And you won't consider it?' Louise's tone switched to appeal.

But Marchand was adamant, responding with dry sarcasm, 'Not unless I go barking mad, in which case I'd want you to have me committed first.'

'Very funny.' Louise pulled a face at her brother's sour humour. 'Well, I hope you'll at least be polite and give her an interview.'

'If I must.' He sighed heavily, then apparently consulted his watch as he ran on, 'Always assuming she turns up. It's already twenty past the hour.'

'Yes, I wonder where she's got...?' Louise trailed off, her question answered as she looked from her brother to the open French windows and caught sight of Clare.

Her face mirrored her shock, then dismay, but her brother didn't notice as he went on, 'Well, if she doesn't materialise soon, I won't even interview her.'

'Fen...' His sister tried to alert him to Clare's presence, while casting an apologetic glance in her direction.

'No, I'm sorry,' Fenwick continued regardless, 'if your pet safe-robber can't be bothered to show up on time——'

'*Fen!*' Louise whispered his name fiercely, at the same time nodding towards the window.

He must have finally caught on, as Clare saw a figure rise from the chair a second before she decided to cut and run herself. She didn't literally run, but walked quickly away, believing neither would be anxious to follow.

She was wrong. Marchand not only followed but, when his shouted, 'Hold on!' was ignored, caught up in a few strides and grabbed at her arm.

Forced to turn, Clare came face to face with Fenwick Marchand for the first time. It was a shock.

She had expected him to be of the same age as Louise—about fifty. But he was much nearer forty. She'd also expected him to look like his voice—bloodless, pompous and self-righteous. She couldn't believe this tall, fair, beautiful man could be a scholarly professor of politics.

He mirrored her look of disbelief. What had he expected? A woman with a number stamped across her forehead?

In some ways Clare had changed little during her three years in prison. Now twenty-six, she still had the small, gamine features that made her look young for her age. And, though her once abundant mass of red hair had been ruthlessly cropped short, the boyish cut emphasised that youthfulness. But she was too thin and too hard-eyed to be considered a beauty any more.

Marchand continued to stare at her until he felt her pulling at his grip, then he muttered, 'I'm not going to apologise, you know.'

'No one asked you to,' Clare responded coldly.

'You shouldn't have been eavesdropping,' he went on. 'It's normal to come to the front door of a house.'

'I did,' Clare spat back. 'Here!'

She shoved the lion door-knocker in his hand. He stared at it in puzzlement.

'Where did you get this?'

'From your front door, and no, I wasn't pinching it,' she said before he could suggest such a thing. 'It came off in my hand.'

'How odd,' he commented, still frowning.

She retorted, 'Not really. Someone had already unscrewed it from its plate.'

'Ah.' Enlightenment dawned on Fenwick Marchand. 'I think I can guess who. I'll see he's punished.'

'Don't bother on my account.' Clare shrugged. 'He's saved us both time.'

'What do you mean?' the man demanded.

'You won't have to go through the motions of an interview now,' Clare explained, 'and I won't have to make a wasted effort to impress you. I'll leave you to square things with Louise,' she concluded briskly, and would have walked away if he hadn't tightened his grip on her arm.

'Hold on,' he protested. 'You can't just walk off like this.'

'Why not?' Clare rallied.

'Well...I mean to say...you have come for an interview, after all,' he argued, somewhat inarticulately for a professor.

'You're not about to offer me a job, are you?' Clare challenged point-blank, and, at his lack of response, added, 'So, there's not much more to say.'

Again she tried to walk away and again he stopped her, muttering, 'You're making me out to be very narrow-minded. I'm not.'

'Really?' Clare's tone suggested she couldn't care less what he was like.

His lips thinned slightly. 'Look, if it were just me, I'd be willing to give you a chance, but I need someone who'll also keep an eye on my son and, frankly——'

'You don't want me teaching him safe-cracking,' Clare cut in abruptly. 'Yes, I know. I heard.'

His lips thinned even more. 'Actually, I was about to comment on your age. My sister led me to believe that you were in your late twenties.'

'I'm twenty-six,' Clare declared.

He was clearly surprised. 'You don't look it.'

'I *can* prove it.'

'I wasn't saying you were lying...' he sighed at her surliness '...merely that you seem much younger... Look, why don't we go inside and discuss the matter over tea?'

Clare shrugged once more. 'Is there any point, Mr Marchand? You've made your opinions clear enough. You won't employ an ex-con and who's to blame you? If it makes you feel any better, I wouldn't employ me either,' she admitted with dark humour.

Surprisingly it drew a smile from the man. 'You're honest, at any rate.'

'That's not what the judge thought,' Clare said in the same flippant vein, showing the hardness that had got her through three years in prison.

'Yes, well,' Marchand continued, 'my sister tells me you're innocent... Are you?'

His directness was disconcerting but oddly it made Clare like him better. Not enough, however, to volunteer her life story.

'Possibly,' she replied on a cryptic note.

'And possibly not?' He lifted an enquiring brow, but she just stared back at him without expression. 'You don't give away much, Miss... what *is* your name?'

'Anderson.'

'Miss Anderson.' He inclined his head as if they were just meeting, then, curling his fingers round her elbow, began steering her back towards the house.

A swift dig in the ribs might have secured her release but Clare had no taste for scenes. She'd already had more than enough drama for one day.

Louise Carlton was waiting for them at the front door. 'I'm terribly sorry, dear.' The older woman smiled in apology. 'I'm not sure how much you heard, but you mustn't take it to heart. It's just Fen's way. He doesn't mean half of it. Do you?' she appealed to her brother.

He contradicted her utterly. 'I wouldn't have said it if I hadn't meant it, and there's no point in pretending otherwise. Miss Anderson isn't a fool... Are you?' he directed at Clare.

'I try not to be,' she answered drily, and it drew the merest flicker of a smile from him.

'So, Lou,' he continued to his sister, 'if you could possibly have tea brought into the study, I'll talk to Miss Anderson there.'

'I... yes, fine.' Louise's eyes questionned Clare as to what was happening. Clare spread her hands in a gesture that said she didn't know, before following him to the far end of the hall.

His study was a very masculine room, decorated in sombre dark colours and dominated by a large leather-bound desk covered in papers. He sat down behind it and waved Clare into the chair opposite. She sat reluctantly.

He slipped on a pair of horn-rimmed glasses. They still failed to make him professorial. He had the looks of an actor, a hybrid of Robert Redford and Charles Dance. Clare thought it just as well he had neither man's charm.

Pen in hand, he asked her point-blank, 'Now, what experience have you of running a house?'

'Not much,' she admitted, then, before he could go on, said, 'Look, I realise you're giving me this interview because you promised Mrs Carlton, but I'd prefer not to bother. You don't wish to hire someone with a prison record. I accept that. I'll be able to catch an earlier train back to London.'

'You're very blunt, aren't you?' He leaned back in his chair and surveyed her, before asking, 'Where do you live in London?'

Clare didn't see the relevance of the question, but answered it all the same. 'Kennington.'

'In a flat?'

'No, in a hostel ... for ex-offenders.'

'What's it like?' he enquired with passing curiosity.

'A palace,' she replied sardonically, resenting his interest.

He pulled a face. 'Is there nowhere else you can go? Friends? Relatives?'

Clare shook her head.

'How long have you lived there?' he pursued.

'Since I was released,' she told him, 'a week ago.'

'And presumably you can stay there till you've arranged alternative accommodation,' he concluded, wrongly.

Clare shook her head again. 'There's a three-month limit.'

'So what happens if you haven't found anywhere else?' He frowned.

She shrugged. She hadn't let herself think that far. 'I'll manage,' she said on a defensive note.

But he wouldn't let it go. 'You won't if you end up on the streets,' he stated grimly. 'No job, no home. It's a vicious circle.'

Clare's eyes narrowed at this little lecture. What did he know about it? 'I'll survive,' she claimed with the hard confidence of someone who'd already been there.

'I suppose you will,' he said, giving her another measuring look that wasn't entirely pleasant. 'A good-looking woman never needs to starve.'

Arguably it was a compliment, but not the way he said it. Mr Fen Marchand clearly didn't have a very high opinion of women.

Clare didn't care enough to argue the point and remained silent. Let someone else deal with his hang-ups.

'You certainly don't seem too anxious to get this job, Miss Anderson.' He switched back to his normal pomposity. 'So far, you've said little to impress . . . You have no experience of running a house, and I don't suppose you have any experience of handling wilful eleven-year-olds?'

Clare shook her head, then, recalling what Louise had told her, enquired, 'Did your last housekeeper?'

'As a matter of fact, she did,' he announced crisply, 'being a widowed lady with three grown-up sons.'

'And how long was she with you?' Clare already knew the answer.

'I . . . well . . . I don't think that's relevant.' He evaded the admission that the last incumbent had lasted a fortnight. 'It seemed she had a weak heart and found the housework more of a strain than she'd anticipated.'

I bet, Clare muttered to herself, thinking of two reasons alone that might have hastened the woman's departure: Marchand senior and his abrasive manner, and Marchand junior and his taste for pranks.

'Anyway, Mrs Brown isn't the issue,' he said dismissively and rose from behind his desk.

Clare assumed the interview was at an end, but, when she made to stand, he waved her back in her seat. 'I'm just going to see where Louise has got with the afternoon tea.'

Clare started to say, I think I should just go, but he'd left the room before she could get the words out. Rude man. She was left twiddling her thumbs and wondering if she shouldn't give everybody a break and leave by the study's French windows.

She was actually contemplating it when a figure blocked her escape route. He stood at the open window for a moment, staring at her, before deciding to enter.

'Where's my old man?' he demanded in a manner so arrogant that his parentage couldn't be doubted. The origin of his blond good looks was also fairly evident. The only difference between the two was one of accent—

while Fen Marchand spoke with a perfect BBC accent, Miles had a slight American drawl.

'I've no idea,' Clare answered him offhandedly. She made no attempt to engage him in further conversation.

The young boy wasn't discouraged. Instead he went round to sit behind his father's desk. 'Has he offered you the job yet?'

This time Clare didn't answer, looking straight through him instead.

'No? Well, I wouldn't take it if he does,' the boy advised. 'The pay's lousy, for a start, and my dad's an even lousier boss. As for me, I can't help it. I'm disturbed, personality-wise.'

'You do surprise me,' Clare said, irony in her tone.

It was lost on the boy. 'I should have an analyst. All the kids in L.A. have an analyst, but my dad's too mean to pay for one.'

'Really?' Clare sounded less than interested in this information. She didn't have too much sympathy for poor little rich boys—not any more.

Miles Marchand frowned at her reaction. He was trying to shock, not bore his audience.

He tried again. 'So, tell me, do you have the hots for him?'

'What?' Clare blinked at the leap in conversation.

'My dad, do you have the hots for him?' he repeated patiently. 'That's what they say in America. It means——'

'I know what it means, and most certainly not!' Clare denied, angered for the first time.

'OK, OK. Keep your hair on.' Miles Marchand shrugged off his suggestion. 'I was only asking. Lots of women do. The last housekeeper but one was crazy about him.'

'So, what did you do to her?' Clare decided it was time to go on the offensive with this monster. 'Frogs in the bed? Dead mice on the doorstep?'

'Don't be stupid,' he dismissed, 'that's kid's stuff. I was much more subtle.'

'Oh, yes?' Clare lifted a sceptical brow. 'Don't tell me, you just concentrated on being as rude and obnoxious as possible, and that did the trick. Well, I wouldn't bother wasting your talents on me, kiddo.'

'Why not?' he demanded.

'Well, apart from the fact I'm tougher and meaner than you could ever hope to be,' Clare claimed extravagantly, 'it's not likely your dad's going to employ me.'

'Why not?' the boy repeated.

Clare was tempted to tell him. She was sure the boy would be thrilled to have a real live criminal in the house.

She eventually said, 'I haven't the right qualifications.'

'Oh, that's no problem,' the boy replied airily. 'He's so desperate, he'll take anyone.'

'Thanks,' muttered Clare and the boy grinned wickedly.

Marchand caught the grin as he returned to the study with a tray of tea things. 'Miles, what are you doing in here?' he asked rather sternly.

'Nothing.' The boy's face changed to sullenness as he slipped from his father's chair.

'He hasn't been rude to you, has he?' Marchand directed at Clare.

Before she could answer, the boy put in, 'I was just talking to her...wasn't I?'

Clare nodded and volunteered, 'About his life in America.'

The boy shot her a look, half-plea, half-threat, and a small smile played on her lips as she kept him on tenterhooks for a moment, before she gave a slight shake of her head.

The man's eyes switched from one to the other, picking up messages but unable to interpret them.

'Well, Miles, I haven't finished interviewing Miss—
er—yet,' he finally said. 'Your aunt has tea ready for
you in the kitchen.'

'OK.' The boy shrugged, then said to Clare, 'Catch
you later, maybe,' as he slouched from the room.

Clare wondered what he meant, what the grin on his
face promised. Nothing good, she suspected.

Marchand looked bemused, saying with near wonder,
'He seems to like you.'

'I wouldn't be too sure.' Clare suspected the boy liked
noboby right at that moment—including himself. She
didn't know if he was disturbed, but he was certainly
mixed-up and unhappy.

'No, well...he can be a handful,' Marchand admitted in something of an understatement, before he
poured tea into two cups and left Clare to help herself
to milk and sugar.

Clare did so as he went on, 'You see, Miles has been
through a difficult time. His mother...she and I parted
seven years ago. Miles stayed with me for the first three
years, then he went to live with her... She died in an
accident six months ago.'

Marchand relayed this information reluctantly, and
Clare realised there was a whole lot more he wasn't
saying. But she showed no curiosity and didn't invite
him to continue. The truth was she didn't want to know
about Miles Marchand's problems. She had enough of
her own.

'He's not the easiest of children in consequence,'
Marchand concluded, 'and needs careful handling.
However, I should be spending much of my time round
the house until autumn term begins and I intend to or-
ganise activities for the boy. I would expect a housekeeper to supervise him occasionally, along with the
normal household duties... So, any questions?'

'No.' Clare saw no point in asking questions. He wasn't
going to employ her. Why should he?

'None?' He frowned at her apparent uninterest, and, when she remained silent, added shortly, 'In that case, if you leave your address, I'll let you know, Miss...'

'All right.' She stood up, placed her half-finished tea on the tray, and surprised him by offering her hand to shake.

'I'll show you out,' he said, when she started to turn and walk from the room.

'That's OK.' Clare would happily have found her own way to the front door, but he followed behind her.

They'd reached the doorstep before he asked, 'How did you get here? By car?'

'No, train, then bus,' Clare answered him.

'In that case——' he took a set of keys from his pocket '——I'd better run you into Oxford.'

'You don't have to.' Clare had decided that, all in all, she didn't particularly like Fenwick Marchand.

'I know I don't,' he responded, 'but nevertheless I will. Wait here till I tell Louise.'

Clare wasn't given the chance to argue as he retreated back into the house. She was left standing on the doorstep, wondering which car was his—the Jaguar or the Mercedes. She was putting her money on the Jaguar when Marchand junior reappeared.

'Why didn't you tell him?' he asked with narrowed eyes.

'Tell him what?'

'That I was rude to you.'

'Were you?' Clare gave him a look of mock-surprise. 'I didn't notice.'

'You must know some incredibly rude people, then,' he threw back at her.

'Incredibly,' she agreed, her smile ironic as she thought of her companions over the last few years. It was true. Manners had been in short supply in Marsh Green Prison.

The boy smiled a little, too, before saying, 'They're arguing about you in the kitchen. Him and Aunt Lou.'

'Really?' Clare said flatly. It wasn't an invitation for him to go on.

But he didn't need one, taking pleasure in confiding, 'They sent me to watch TV in the lounge, but I hung around and listened at the door. Aunt Lou says you're really desperate for this job and he has to give you a chance. But he says you don't strike him as especially desperate and that a girl with your talents will have much more luc—luc-ar-tive prospects lined up... I guess he means you're too smart to just be a housekeeper,' Miles interpreted for her.

But Clare could think of an entirely different interpretation, and it was nowhere near that flattering. Inwardly seething, she muttered at the boy, 'Something like that,' then told him to inform his father she had chosen to walk.

She left without waiting for a response from the boy but he caught up with her on the drive and fell into step beside her.

'Are you mad with me?' he enquired guilelessly. 'I thought you'd want to know what they were saying. I mean, if you told Dad you *were* desperate, perhaps he'd change his mind.'

'I doubt it.' Clare decided that, for all the worldliness he affected, Miles Marchand had a boy's outlook on life. She wondered if she might have liked him, had she been given the chance.

'You could try,' he insisted as they reached the gates.

Clare shook her head. 'Don't worry about it, kid. It'll save you the trouble of scaring me off,' she said with a wry smile.

'But you wouldn't be,' Miles responded. '*You're* not scared of me, are you?'

Clare shook her head again, saying, 'No. Should I be?'

'The rest were,' he claimed. 'Mrs Brown, the last woman, she told him I needed locking up. In a loony-bin, she meant.'

Clare frowned, not sure if the boy was exaggerating, boasting or just seeking her opinion. 'What do you think?' she asked in return.

The boy stared at her for a moment, deciding if she could be trusted, before he confided, 'I scare myself sometimes. I feel so angry I want to hurt people. Him especially.'

'Your dad?' Clare drew a nod, then found herself admitting, 'I used to feel that way at times.'

'So what did you do?' Dark blue eyes looked to her for an answer.

Clare had none to give. All the people close to her had gone, out of reach of hurting, and she'd resolved her anger with the world by retreating from it. But this boy still had a chance to come out of the shadows.

'I'm nobody to take advice from, kid,' she finally said, and felt a twinge of guilt when his expression became hostile once more. He'd opened up to her, just for a moment, and what did she do? Turn her back on him.

She did it literally, as she slipped out through the gates and started walking back along the country road to the Old Corn Mill. However, she didn't get very far before the Jaguar drew up beside her.

The driver's window slid down and Marchand senior's dark blond head appeared. 'If you're intending to catch a bus, there isn't one for a couple of hours. So, I suggest you get in,' he said with a bored air.

It put Clare's back up. 'I'd sooner walk, thank you,' she replied heavily.

He arched a brow. 'Twelve miles? You must be joking. You won't make three. Still, if you insist...' He turned on the engine and put the car in gear, then waited for Clare to forget her pride and be sensible.

But she remained where she was, waiting in turn, until finally he put his foot on the accelerator and shot off down the road.

Clare felt triumphant until she reached the pub at the crossroads and saw the sign that indeed said it was twelve miles to Oxford. Then she wondered if she could walk all that way on new court shoes that were already beginning to pinch.

She was tempted to hitch-hike, but didn't. A car stopped of its own accord while she stood there.

'Going to Oxford?' the young man driving the open-topped Morgan enquired, and, at her nod, invited, 'Hop in.'

Clare hesitated, but not for long. The young man had Hooray Henry written all over him and she judged him—if not his driving—to be safe.

She was right. He drove like an idiot, chatted her up like mad, but made no dangerous moves. She earned her lift by listening, more or less attentively, to his bad jokes, suffered his laughter and thanked him politely for delivering her direct to the station.

She'd no sooner waved him goodbye than a car screeched up in his place. A Jaguar, green in colour, familiar in driver.

She was so surprised, she waited while Fen Marchand jumped out of his car and, with a face like thunder, came round to her side.

'And who was that?' he demanded without preamble. 'A friend of yours?'

'Well, no...' Clare found herself on the defensive. 'Not a friend, exactly. He just offered me a lift.'

'I know,' he grated back. 'The question is what he imagined *you* were offering in return.'

'I...nothing!' Clare spluttered back. 'Look, Mr Marchand, I don't know what kind of girl you think I am——'

'The stupid kind,' he cut in rudely. 'Forget the fact he was driving like a bloody maniac most of the way. Do you know how many places he could have turned off on that road? Do you?' he demanded, grasping her roughly by the arms.

Unable to free herself, Clare threw back, 'You tell me. You're the one that goes creeping around, following people.'

'I was waiting in the pub car park for you,' he countered heavily, 'when you decided to go off with a total stranger. What do you expect me to do? Leave you to get raped on some lonely farm track?' he said brutally.

The words made Clare flinch, then relent slightly. 'In that case, it's kind of you to be concerned, but I *can* take care of myself.'

'I bet!' He scoffed at the idea, before coldly informing her, 'It wasn't kindness, Miss Anderson, it was self-preservation. I didn't fancy being suspect number one had your lift decided to murder you in a post-coital rage,' he declared with angry volume.

Clare's face flamed like an over-ripe tomato, conscious of heads turning in their direction. 'Would you keep your voice down?'

'Why?' he threw back at her. 'I imagine you like people noticing you. Young men, at any rate. In fact, I wonder if I misjudged the situation. Perhaps you were *hoping* for a little adventure down some country lane——'

'Why, you——' Clare tore her arm free and cracked a hand against his cheek.

He touched his face, shocked for an instant, then rasped, 'You bitch!' as he made a grab for her again.

She backed off, hissing at him, 'You want me to scream, Professor...? Do you?'

Fenwick Marchand looked angry enough not to care. He took a step towards her and she opened her mouth as if to scream. 'All right,' he growled at her, 'you win. Don't make a fool of us both.'

'Oh, you don't need any help for that, Professor,' she retorted on a contemptuous note that drew his furious scowl.

'Then presumably you don't need my help either, Miss Anderson,' he countered in a voice like ice.

'If you mean your job—stick it!' Clare suggested less than politely, and, having burned her boats, walked off into the rush-hour crowd.

She felt good. Buoyant. Triumphant. At least until she'd caught her train. Then she had time to think, time to count the cost of another failure. True, she'd never stood a chance. He had written her off before they'd even met. But he wasn't going to be the only one. Few people wanted to employ ex-offenders.

And that was what she was. Clare Mary Anderson. Number 67904, C Wing, H.M. Prison, Marsh Green, Sussex. Category B prisoner. Convicted of a variety of offences.

Guilty of some, too.

CHAPTER TWO

'LOUISE!' Clare was taken aback at the sight of the other woman standing outside her room in the hostel.

'I did telephone,' Louise Carlton explained, 'but there was no answer.'

'No, the caretaker's hardly ever there,' Clare answered absently, still staring in surprise at her visitor.

It had been over two weeks since the interview. She hadn't heard from Fenwick Marchand or Louise in that time, but then she hadn't really expected to. She'd assumed Marchand would relay their quarrel and his sister would naturally take his side.

But here was Louise, saying in her kindly manner, 'I meant to come last week, only I had a touch of flu... May I come in?'

'Yes, of course.' Clare waved her inside the room and cleared her only chair of a bag of shopping so that the older woman could sit down. 'I was going to write to apologise, but...'

'Apologise?' Louise looked quizzical.

'Well, I know I let you down.' That had been Clare's main concern over that fiasco of an interview. Louise had given her a chance, and she'd done her best to blow it.

'On the contrary,' Louise rejoined, 'it's I who should apologise. I hadn't realised my brother could be so narrow-minded. I should have, though. He's never been easy, even as a small boy.'

Clare could believe that, although she found it hard to imagine Fen Marchand as anything but fully grown and mean with it.

'He was a late baby,' Louise confided, 'and tragically our mother died shortly after his birth. Fen's upbringing

25

was left to a series of housekeepers, before our father packed him off to prep school at the age of eight.'

Clare was struck by the similarity between Marchand senior's childhood and Marchand junior's. 'Is Miles at boarding-school, too?'

Louise shook her head. 'Fen has been educating him at home, but boarding-school is definitely on the cards. He's at his wits' end, you see. That's why I'm here...'

Clare frowned, wondering what Louise was leading up to. Surely Marchand wasn't considering employing her?

It seemed not as Louise ran on, 'I might as well be frank. He took on another housekeeper last week when I was ill. He got her through an agency. Anyway...' She hesitated mid-tale.

Clare misunderstood, saying, 'It's all right, Louise. I knew he'd never offer *me* the job. I don't mind.'

'Oh, but he *is*,' Louise insisted, 'offering you the job. Now. If you'll take it... You haven't got another, have you?'

'Well, no, but...' Clare had lost the thread of this conversation somewhere '...if he has someone else?'

'*Had*,' Louise corrected drily. 'She lasted two days. I'm afraid Miles didn't take to her and, well...I might as well tell you—he put a frog in her bed. A dead one. I know it sounds absolutely disgusting. Actually it was. But I can honestly say he's never done anything quite like it before. Been rude, certainly, and answered back, but nothing quite like that. I don't know where he got such an idea from.'

Clare did. She remembered giving it to him.

'Fen was livid,' Louise continued, 'and duly announced that Miles was to go to boarding-school in the autumn, whether he liked it or not. Well, Miles obviously doesn't like it because he's been in a state of dumb misery ever since.'

'Oh.' Clare's face clouded in sympathy with the boy.

'Not that I blame Fen,' Louise hastened to add. 'What else can he do? He can't work and look after Miles, and it's too late for him to take a year's sabbatical. He's tried.'

'Really?' Clare didn't hide her surprise. Because he was well-off and successful, she hadn't seen Fen Marchand in the role of a single parent, struggling to do the right thing for his son.

'He doesn't say so, but I know he feels guilty,' Louise confided. 'He thinks he's letting Miles down again, although what could he have done the first time?'

'The first time?' Clare echoed automatically.

'When Diana won custody of Miles,' Louise explained, before asking her, 'Fen did tell you about his wife, didn't he?'

'Not really.' Clare didn't think Fen Marchand was the type for confidences. His sister, however, had no such reservations.

'They met at Oxford. Diana was an undergraduate while Fen was working for his doctorate,' she ran on. 'She was very beautiful, Diana. Head-turning, you might say. Quite clever, too, I suppose. It was the first and last time Fen acted on impulse. He married her within six months of their meeting...' Louise paused to shake her head over the fact.

Clare kept quiet, unable to visualise a Fen Marchand who acted on impulse.

'Unfortunately Miles came along after a year,' Louise added, 'and motherhood was the last thing Diana was suited to. Miles was barely a month old when she disappeared on a cruise with her rich father, leaving Fen and Miles to look after themselves. That pretty much set the pattern for the next five years until she bowed out altogether.'

'But she fought for Miles's custody,' Clare replied, frowning.

'Only at her father's insistence,' Louise revealed. 'A self-made man, he wanted a male heir to take over his

electronics firm. He footed her legal bill, and, unbelievably, some idiot judge decided Miles would be better
off with his mother. So, after spending eight years of
his life at Woodside, the boy suddenly found himself
living in South Kensington with his grandfather.'

'Not his mother?' Clare was a little lost.

'Officially, yes——' Louise pulled a face '—but, by
that time, Diana was following her latest boyfriend round
the polo circuit. *Fen* saw the boy more often on access
visits. It was hell for him. He could see old man Derwent
ruining Miles as he had ruined Diana, but could do little
about it.

'Then disaster really struck,' Louise went on un-
happily. 'Derwent died and that left Diana with custody.
She might have handed Miles back, only Derwent left
the bulk of his fortune to the boy in trust, and where
he went control of his trust went.'

'So she kept him,' Clare concluded, her heart going
out to the boy caught in the middle.

Louise nodded. 'Fen was disraught. He didn't trust
Diana to take care of him properly and immediately filed
for custody. Diana countered by whisking Mikes away
abroad.'

'To America?' Clare recalled Miles saying he'd lived
in L.A.

'Via Australia and South America,' Louise recounted. 'Diana spent six months country-hopping, with
Miles as excess baggage, while Fen desperately tried to
locate them long enough to get a court order im-
plemented, forcing her to return the boy to the UK.'

Once more Clare was surprised. From their brief encounter, she'd thought Fen Marchand almost indifferent
to his son.

Louise read her mind, and claimed, 'They'd been so
close, Miles and his father, but their years apart have
done untold damage. Miles feel his father let him down,
and, I suspect, Fen feels the same. He wants to make it
up to him, but doesn't want to spoil him in the process...

Which sort of brings me to the point of my visit,' Louise concluded finally. 'As Miles plainly loathes the idea of boarding-school, Fen asked him what *would* make him happy? And you'll never guess what he said!'

While Louise paused for effect, Clare guessed the truth. She just didn't believe it.

'Well...' Louise could hardly contain her satisfaction '...it seems Miles took a real shine to you, Clare, and he's promised that if you were to come and housekeep for them he'd be on his absolutely best behaviour. Can you credit it?' The older woman smiled as if something miraculous had occurred.

Clare didn't see it that way. If she held some appeal for the boy, it was a momentary thing and based on all the wrong reasons. He saw her as a fellow traveller, at odds with the rest of the world. She wouldn't dispute that—but it hardly made her a candidate for the role of Mary Poppins.

'How did the professor react?' she asked point-blank.

'Well...he was taken aback,' Louise admitted carefully, and Clare's lips spread in a thin smile as she imagined how taken aback Marchand would have been. 'However,' Louise added quickly, 'he's come round to the idea now.'

'The idea?'

'Of your being housekeeper.'

Clare still couldn't take it in. Marchand was willing to give her the job to please his son?

'He feels he may not have been very fair to you on the day of the interview,' Louise relayed, 'and he's prepared to give you a month's trial. What do you think?'

The older woman's smile said she expected Clare to be grateful for the opportunity.

Because she liked Louise Carlton, Clare forced a smile in return. But inside she wondered how the other woman had managed to reach the age of fifty-odd and remain one of life's innocents. Didn't she realise that this was just a way of Marchand hiring her until the boy got over

his 'fancy' for her? When that happened, she'd be out
the door quicker than she could say 'month's trial'.

'You'll have your own little flat in the house,' Louise
went on persuasively, 'with shower, kitchenette and television, and a salary of eight thousand pounds plus keep.'

'Eight thousand pounds?' Clare was shocked by the
amount.

Louise misunderstood. 'Yes, it didn't seem much to
me, either, but at least you wouldn't have living ex-
penses,' she pointed out.

'It's fine,' Clare assured her quickly. 'In fact, it's much
more than I expected, with my not having any real
experience.'

'Well, don't worry.' Louise smiled again. 'Fen can
afford it. He has a considerable private income as well
as his professor's salary.'

'Really?' Clare wasn't altogether surprised at this.
Although the house was not ostentatiously large, the
sheer understated elegance of Woodside Hall whispered
money. Old money, if Clare wasn't very much mistaken.

'When does he want me to start?' she asked Louise.

'Oh, as soon as you can,' Louise said with obvious
relief. 'I'm holding the fort at present, but I just *have*
to return to London this week. There are so many things
I should have done, only I was ill.'

'You work too hard.' Clare had some idea of Louise's
busy timetable of voluntary work from their conver-
sations in prison.

Clare remembered how she herself had been
unenthusiastic about her visits at first, but had come to
like and respect Louise Carlton. She realised that it had
been an act of faith for Louise to suggest her for this
job.

'I can start immediately,' she declared resolutely, and
drew a beaming smile in response. 'I'll just pack.'

'Are you sure?' Louise protested for form's sake. 'I'll
drive you up with your cases.'

'It's all right,' Clare replied. 'I only have the one. I can go by train.'

'One case?' Louise watched with concern as the younger woman packed all her worldly possessions into a single battered suitcase. 'My dear girl, you're going to need some more clothes. We'll shop on the way.'

Clare shook her head, saying simply, 'I have no money.'

'Never mind. My treat!' Louise announced with her usual generosity.

Clare shook her head again. 'Thanks very much, but I'll wait till I get my wages and buy something.'

'Clare,' the older woman pursued, 'please let me get you something. I can easily afford it and I'd enjoy having someone young and pretty to dress for a change.'

'It's very kind of you, but I'd really prefer not. The only thing I might need is an apron or overall, for the housekeeping, and there's probably one at the house.'

'Possibly, but, going on Fen's previous choices of housekeeper, any garment will go round you twice.' Louise frowned a little as she assessed Clare's extremely slim figure.

Clare shrugged in response. She knew how she looked—thin to the point of skinniness, shaped more like a boy than a woman. Once she would have cared. Once she'd been like any teenage girl, preening herself in the mirror, dressing to attract the boys—or at least one particular boy. And where had it led, all that wishing and hoping, believing her looks could get her anything?

Clare's face hardened, reflecting her thoughts, and Louise added softly, 'I wish you'd let me help ... really help.'

'You have. You've got me this job.'

'I didn't mean that. I wish you'd open up a little, tell me about yourself.'

Louise reached out a hand to touch her arm. It was plainly a gesture of compassion and understanding, but it took an effort on Clare's part not to shrug off the gentle hand. She didn't want to open up. She wanted to stay as she was, locked up tight, safe from thought or feeling.

'You know why I was in prison,' she responded evenly as she returned to her packing.

Louise Carlton dropped her hand away, recognising rejection, but persevered. 'Yes, I know. I just find it impossible to believe you did such a thing. That's why I haven't told Fen yet...' she finished in gentle warning.

'But what if he asks me?' Clare worried. 'He's bound to want to know why I was in prison.'

'Yes, well...I did say you'd been convicted of stealing,' Louise admitted, 'but that was all. I feel we should wait to tell him the rest.'

'If you think so.' Clare left the decision to Louise, seeing no alternative. They both knew full well that, if the brother were to find out the truth, Clare would be shown the door.

As it was, she travelled up to Oxford with Louise Carlton that afternoon, almost positive that her stay at Woodside Hall would be brief and fraught enough, without the added complication of true confessions.

'Fen *is* going to be surprised when he sees you,' Louise said, when they finally drew up outside the Georgian manor house.

The big oak door opened just as they climbed out of the car. Fen Marchand stood on the threshold, ignoring Louise's smile of greeting, looking past her to Clare.

To say he was surprised was an understatement. Shocked or, possibly, horrified was nearer the mark, Clare thought.

'Well, brother, dear,' Louise spoke first, 'are you just going to stare at the poor girl or are you going to welcome her to Woodside Hall?'

For a moment longer it seemed that Fen Marchand was going to do just that—stare at her—as he continued to stand there, motionless. Then he took his sister's hint and, leaving the doorway, approached Clare.

Dark-suited the last time they'd met, today he was dressed in a polo shirt and casual trousers. Tall and muscular, he was built more like an athlete than a college professor, but his voice and manner were those of a dry-as-dust intellectual.

'Miss Anderson,' he addressed her formally, 'I assume my sister has informed you about your terms and conditions, and so forth?'

'Yes...thank you.' Clare kept her tone equally neutral.

'Very well,' he continued, 'you may start to-morrow...if that's acceptable?'

'Yes, fine,' she nodded in response.

'Good, then I'll show you to your room. Have you brought any luggage?' he asked abruptly.

Clare nodded again. 'It's in the boot.'

Louise, keeping her distance till then, appeared with the keys. 'Here, Fen, you fetch Clare's case while I show her the attic you're exiling her to. Come on.' She smiled invitingly at Clare and led the way inside.

Clare followed with some reluctance. Although Fen Marchand had been polite and correct to her, it was just a façade. She hadn't forgotten their last encounter at the railway station, and neither had he.

She felt his eyes boring into her back as she walked through the front door and, despite the heat of the day, shivered in the marble-tiled hall, before following Louise up the wide staircase to the galleried landing of the first floor. They passed a series of rooms, turned a corner into another corridor and went to the door at the far end. It opened out into a much narrower staircase.

Clare began to have visions of dust and darkness, with a single bed for furniture and, perhaps, if she was lucky, a candle to read by. But it seemed she'd been reading too many novels in the prison library. She was quite taken aback when they arrived at their destination.

It wasn't so much a room as an open-plan flat, with a living area at one end and a bedroom plus shower cubicle at the other. It was furnished in genuine antique pine, with a polished wooden floor, rug-scattered, and a large old-fashioned sofa upholstered in blue velvet. Light streamed in from a series of skylights and heat was provided by a fairly modern gas heater inset in the wall.

'A bit of a climb, I'm afraid,' Louise apologised as Clare looked round the room.

'I didn't expect ... anything like this.' Clare's uncertainty hid her delight in the place. After prison and the hostel, it seemed unreal.

'Yes, well, the only trouble is the lack of toilet,' Louise said, still in an apologetic vein. 'You'll have to go downstairs for that. A dreadful inconvenience, I know, but at least you'll have a bit of privacy up here.'

'It's absolutely wonderful,' Clare assured the older woman, her smile showing she meant it. 'I just didn't expect anywhere so nice.'

Louise smiled in response. 'Well, I'm glad you like it. It used to be the servants' quarters in bygone times—a rather dingy, depressing place—but Fen had it refurbished for my son Gerry to board in while he was up at Oxford. I don't think it has had any use since.'

Clare frowned, wondering if she'd understood correctly. 'What about the other housekeepers? Didn't they stay here?'

Louise looked embarrassed for a moment as she shook her head. 'Well, no, most of them have lived out, or occupied a couple of adjoining rooms on the first floor ... but Fen thought you might prefer up here.' Louise's hesitancy cast doubt over her brother's motives.

Clare was quite sure Fen Marchand couldn't care less about her preferences. It seemed much more likely that it was his own privacy he was protecting. Having opened his house to a convicted criminal, he'd decided to isolate her as far as possible from the rest of the household.

Well, Clare didn't object. She'd clean his house and cook his meals as efficiently as she could, and, when not working, keep to her own company. She had no wish to become a so-called 'part of the family'. Apart from her dislike of Marchand, she believed no housekeeper was ever really such.

Her thoughts went to her own mother. She'd worked for Lord Abbotsford for over fifteen years and her ladyship had often referred to her as 'almost one of the family'. But, even as a child, Clare had known they were just words, empty words. It had simply been a way of claiming Mary Anderson's loyalty. When her mother had become ill with stomach cancer, the Holsteads had been conspicuous by their absence.

Clare's mouth twisted at the memory and it was a bitter expression Fenwick Marchand caught as he walked through the attic door. His eyes narrowed; he was clearly wondering what she was thinking, scheming...

Then Louise turned and spotted him, saying, 'This was a good idea of yours, Fen. Clare loves it. Don't you, Clare?'

'Yes,' Clare answered as promised, but her tone was leaden.

Not surprisingly, Fen Marchand looked sceptical. 'I must say you contain your enthusiasm very well, Miss Anderson,' he muttered in dry sarcasm.

It wasn't lost on Clare but neither was his position as her boss; she managed to contain her temper.

It was Louise who said, 'Don't be such a sourpuss, Fen. You don't want to scare off Clare before she's even started, do you?'

From his deadpan gaze, Clare suspected that was exactly what Fen Marchand wanted. When their eyes met and locked, and she refused to look away, he said, 'I don't think Miss Anderson scares so easily.'

'Possibly not——' Louise totally missed the silent exchange of hostilities '—but you could still try to be a little pleasanter. Clare isn't used to your sense of humour, and, if she were to take to her heels, then where would you be?' she asked rhetorically.

Her brother answered her all the same, with a dry, 'Housekeeperless, I presume.'

'Precisely.' Louise felt she'd just made her point. 'And you know you can't manage on your own, Fen, so try to be nice, hmm?' she appealed.

If Fen Marchand's less than nice expression was anything to go by, the appeal fell on deaf ears. But Louise seemed oblivious, taking his silence as assent.

'Good, so that's settled,' she announced with totally unwarranted optimism. 'Now I must dash. I have a charity do this evening and I simply can't miss it... Clare, any problems, just give me a call,' she invited kindly.

'Thank you.' Clare smiled, knowing already what her biggest problem would be.

He chimed in, 'I don't suppose this advice service extends to me?'

Louise gave a brief laugh. 'My dear Fen, the last time you took my advice on anything you were five years old. I can't believe you'll start wanting it now.'

'You never know.' He actually smiled for a moment, but it was solely at his sister and didn't reach the eyes flicking back from her to Clare.

Once more Clare returned his stare, her eyes telling him she understood. She was here only under sufferance and it was going to be no lifelong career.

'Well, you know the number,' Louise replied, and, with a last smile for both of them, stopped her brother from following her by adding, 'No, it's all right. I want a last word with Miles, then I'll show myself out. You stay and tell Clare what her duties are.'

So saying, she went back down the steps, leaving Clare and Fen Marchand to trade hostile stares.

It was he who broke off first, walking past her to place her suitcase on the bed. 'If you give me the address, I'll send for the rest.'

'The rest of what?' Clare was slow on the uptake.

'Your luggage,' he said patiently.

She shook her head. 'There's no more. That's it.'

His eyes widened in surprise. 'You believe in travelling light. Or aren't you planning to stay long?'

'That's up to you, Mr Marchand,' she replied coolly. 'I've brought all my possessions and given up my room at the hostel.'

'In that case,' he countered, 'we'd better try and make this work. Firstly, we need some ground rules.'

'Yes?' Clare waited for him to continue, assuming all the rules were going to be made by him.

'Right.' He slanted his head on one side, studying her for a moment. 'You don't smoke, I hope.'

'No,' she answered simply.

'Good, I can't abide the smell of stale tobacco... What about drink?'

'Drink?'

'Alcohol,' he added with some impatience. 'Do you drink and if so, how much?'

Clare's brows lifted. He certainly believed in being blunt and to the point. 'I haven't had a drink in three years,' she stated with absolute honesty.

He was unimpressed. 'Well, that tells me how long you were in prison,' he commented drily, 'but what about before? Was your crime drink-related?'

'No.' Clare held in a sigh. 'I don't have a drink problem, if that's what you're asking...I don't take drugs, either,' she added, before he could ask any awkward questions on that line. Questions she might not be able to answer honestly.

'You don't smoke. You don't drink. You don't take drugs. So, are there any vices you'd like to admit to?' he asked in a tone that suggested he wasn't taking her word for anything.

Clare gave a shrug that he could read how he liked. She wasn't about to tell him the one vice that had led her to prison—her blind, obsessive love for John Holstead, the son and heir of the fifth Earl of Abbotsford.

'What about men?' He got on to the subject without any help from her. 'Is there some boyfriend in the background?' His lips formed a curve of distaste, as if he

imagined any boyfriend she'd choose would be an un-
savoury character.

It was too much for Clare, trying hard to keep her
temper under control. 'If I have,' she rallied, 'I think
that's my business, Mr Marchand.'

His face darkened at her answer. Free speech was obviously considered his prerogative, and his alone.

'On the contrary,' he argued, 'it would most definitely
be my business should you intend that this boyfriend
visit you here, at my home.'

'Well, I don't,' Clare declared abruptly, meaning to
close the subject.

She felt no obligation to go further and state that there
would be no boyfriend, now or later. She'd only ever
loved one man. She'd worshipped him from the age of
twelve, humiliated herself for him more times than she
cared to remember, made love with him in beds of straw
and backs of cars, and, through everything, remained
blind to the point of stupidity.

'Good.' Fen Marchand's chilly tones brought her back
to the present. 'Because I value my privacy and would
not appreciate it being invaded by some male stranger
staying overnight in my attic. I trust you take my
meaning, Miss Anderson?'

Clare nodded and kept her opinion to herself. She
really didn't want to lose this job before she'd even
begun. She had something to prove first.

'Right, well, you can start tomorrow morning.
Breakfast,' he announced briskly, and had walked past
her to the door before he thought of asking, 'You can
cook, can't you?'

'Just about.' She gave him the answer she felt the
question deserved.

His face clouded over once more, but he said nothing,
as he turned on his heel and marched off downstairs.

Clare could guess what he was thinking. Here he was,
giving a chance to one of his sister's no-hopers, and
getting precious little gratitude in return. He was right,

too. Clare felt nothing towards him except a growing dislike.

But she had to make an effort, Clare told herself, at least try to be the polite, colourless housekeeper he wanted. If only subservience were a more natural part of her character. She grimaced as she thought of her mother. Yes, your ladyship. No, your ladyship. Of course, your ladyship. In all those years, had her mother ever wanted to say, Go to hell, your ladyship?

Possibly she had, but circumstances had made her dependent on the Holsteads. She'd been a nanny to another county family when she'd met Clare's father, Tom Anderson. He'd been an assistant trainer at Lord Abbotsford's racing stables. After a fairly brief courtship, they'd married and were given one of the cottages on the estate. Clare had arrived a year later and, within months of her birth, her father had been killed in a riding accident. Lord Abbotsford had made no offer of financial compensation, but, 'out of the goodness of his heart', had allowed Mary Anderson to remain in the cottage in return for some help in the nursery.

The Holsteads had two children, Sarah and John. Sarah had been two years older than Clare but the two had played together until Sarah had gone away to boarding-school at eleven. Johnny had been five years older and a complete tyrant to the two girls.

Eventually her mother had transferred to the position of housekeeper. At the same time, Clare had grown apart from the children of the house. On the few occasions Sarah or John had been home from school, they'd usually been accompanied by friends and had treated Clare very distantly.

Clare had been a little hurt but understood. She might have the same accent, acquired in those nursery days, and she might dress similarly, albeit in Sarah's discards, but the social gulf between them was a chasm.

It had been different later, when Clare had flowered from an awkward, mop-headed tomboy, with sticks for

legs and a chest flat as a board, to a suddenly beautiful
redhead, with a swan-like neck and a slim, curving figure
and the face of a model, all huge green eyes and hollow
cheeks. Then one of the Holstead children had taken
notice of her again, only this time he hadn't played
tyrant.

Clare caught the drift of her thoughts and stopped
them dead. She wasn't going to go up that road another
time. She had cried enough for Johnny. She wasn't going
to cry any more—not for him or any man.

She bent to start her unpacking. It didn't take long.
Her clothes took up a tiny corner of the wardrobe. She
caught sight of herself in the mirror on the reverse side
of the door and pulled a face. She still appeared young,
remarkably so after three years inside, but her looks had
gone. She was thin to the point of emaciation, like an
anorexic schoolgirl, with a complexion of paste. She recalled how she'd looked the summer she'd turned seventeen, how she'd felt, and for a moment she mourned
the loss of that beauty. Then the film rolled on and she
saw how it had really been a curse, not a gift, and she
called herself a fool for even minding.

She firmly closed the wardrobe door and jumped a
little when she turned to discover herself no longer alone.

'What are you doing here?' she demanded of Miles
Marchand, standing there, quite coolly spying on her.

He shrugged. 'Nothing. Why shouldn't I be here?'

'Because it's my room,' she said very clearly, 'and you
don't come in without an invitation. OK?'

Clare wasn't kidding and she gave him a look that
said as much.

'OK,' Miles muttered back, 'there's no reason to get
uptight. I got you the job, you know,' he claimed in an
arrogant tone, reminiscent of Marchand senior. 'He
didn't want to employ you. He said you were too young.
You don't look particularly young to me.'

'Thanks.' Clare grimaced but didn't take offence. No adult looked young to an eleven-year-old. 'Would you like to sit down?' She sat herself in the wicker chair.

He was slow to accept the invitation but eventually he slouched down on the velvet settee, hands stuck in his pockets. He wanted to make it clear that he was doing her the favour.

'Can you swim?' he asked after a minute's silence.

'Yes.'

'Well?'

'Moderately.'

'Can you bowl?'

'Ten-pin?'

'Yeah.'

'Then no.'

The boy looked disappointed. She'd failed that one.

'I don't suppose you can ride a horse,' he said disdainfully.

'As a matter of fact,' Clare responded, 'I can.'

He looked sceptical, much in the same way his father did. 'A proper horse, I mean. Not a pony or anything.'

'A proper horse,' she echoed, picturing the beautiful animals in the Earl's stables. She'd mucked out, washed down and brushed up, for the privilege of exercising the less important racers.

'I had a horse once,' the boy announced. 'A bay mare.'

'What was her name?' she asked.

'Flash,' he replied. 'She was called that because she was fast. I mean really fast. Her sire was a Derby winner,' he declared proudly.

It was Clare's turn to look sceptical. The fact did not go unnoticed.

'You don't believe me, do you?' he accused. 'But it's true. My grandfather bought her for me. Then *she* sold him.'

'Your mother?' Clare guessed.

He nodded. 'After Grandpa died, she sold everything she could—houses, cars, paintings, the lot, so she could follow Ricky boy round the world.'

'Ricky?' Clare echoed automatically before she realised it might not be a good idea.

'Her boyfriend Ricardo,' he said disdainfully. 'He was an Argentinian polo-player. When he lost a match, he used to beat his horses.'

'Did he hurt you?' she asked quietly.

He pulled a slight face, then shook his head. 'He used to shout at me sometimes. I didn't care. Mostly it was in Spanish and I only know a little . . . He shouldn't have hit his horses, though.'

'No.' Clare agreed with this solemn judgement.

Then he added matter-of-factly, 'Never mind. He's dead now.'

'What?' Clare wondered if she'd heard properly.

'He died in a car crash,' Miles relayed, 'with my mother.'

'Oh,' Clare murmured inadequately, then added a quietly sympathetic, 'You must miss her.'

It drew a belligerent look and an immediate denial. 'No, I don't! Why should I? She didn't care about me.'

Clare shook her head. 'I'm sure she did, Miles. Sometimes grown-ups are too busy with their own lives, but that doesn't mean——'

'What do you know?' Miles cut in abruptly and jumped to his feet. 'You're just a servant!'

It was intended as the ultimate insult but Clare didn't take offence. She could tell from the colour suffusing his face that he regretted his words the moment they were out, but didn't know how to take them back. Instead he turned and ran.

Clare heard him take the stairs two at a time, clattering noisily down the plain wooden treads, and sighed aloud. It hadn't taken her long to upset Miles, and he had been the one to secure her the post. But did she want this job so badly that she was willing to let herself be ruled by the moods of an eleven-year-old boy?

The answer was no, but that wasn't exactly the correct question. She might not *want* the job, but she needed it—at least until she found something else.

Perhaps she should put an advert in the paper:

Female ex-con, twenty-six, with drugs and theft convictions, no good with children, no good at being humble either. Anything considered. Apply Box...

Somehow she didn't think she'd get much response, yet there seemed little point in lying about her past when it would inevitably be found out.

Plainly, this was her best chance. If the Marchands, senior and junior, would just let her get on with the cooking and cleaning, without expecting anything else from her, she could be reasonably content here. She'd work hard for them when on duty, and, when not, she'd escape to her attic sanctuary.

She looked round the room again with an appreciative eye. As bed-sits went, it was beautifully furnished, comfortable without being over-fussy, nothing too valuable to use, but nothing cheap and nasty either. Louise's son had been lucky to have such a place to study in.

Clare stretched out on the bed and, as in prison, let her imagination wander to better things.

How different it would all be if *she'd* come to Oxford to study, not skivvy—to work for a degree that would be her passport to a new life. It wasn't so fanciful. She'd been considered fairly bright at school. She'd gained eight O levels, and gone on to do A levels...only that same year Johnny Holstead had been sent down from university, and her studies had flown out the window, along with her common sense.

She couldn't believe now that she'd been such a fool. To give up a future for a few meaningless words of love and a summer of stolen meetings. He'd never once taken her out, never shown her his world, yet she'd turned her own life upside-down for him, believing he meant his 'forever' promises.

Their engagement had been announced in *The Times*, on September the fourteenth. Clare remembered precisely, because a good part of her had died that day. Their picture had been in the tabloids, too. The Earl of Abbotsford's son, John, was marrying the daughter of a duke, Lady Elizabeth Beaumaris.

Clare had refused to believe it at first. It was she who should have been standing at his side, a smiling, radiant bride-to-be. Not some stuffed dummy of a deb.

Johnny had agreed, even as he'd told her that he had to marry the duke's daughter. Love was one thing, money another, and the Holsteads' declining fortunes required him to take a rich wife. It had always been that way among the upper classes. It didn't have to affect their relationship, he'd explained, seriously expecting Clare to accept the role of mistress.

He'd had no idea how he'd destroyed her life and she hadn't stuck around long enough to tell him. She'd abandoned school and home, and fled to Brighton where she'd found work in a hotel. She'd lost that job five months later and been forced to seek refuge in a women's hostel. She'd kept in touch with her mother but had been unable to return home.

Her eighteenth birthday had come and gone without celebration, unlike Johnny's wedding which had been splashed all over the newspapers. It had finally killed off her dreams. Till then she'd hoped Johnny might break his engagement and come looking for her, his true love. But that only happened in books. In real life, he married the heiress and lived richly ever after.

She'd been twenty-two before she'd returned to Abbotsford Hall. Her mother had fallen ill, the first stage of the cancer that would kill her, and she'd come back to look after her. She'd had no other choice but it had proved a mistake. Having got over Johnny, she'd believed that he too would be happy to ignore her return. Instead it had led to a chain of events that had ended in tragedy for the Holstead family and prison for her.

Now she was starting again, and this time it was going to be different. She neither needed nor desired personal attachments. Prison had equipped her for surviving without such luxuries and she preferred it that way. She'd never love again, or have a child, or tear herself inside out—not for any man.

Nothing was worth that much pain.

CHAPTER THREE

'OH...GOOD morning,' Fen Marchand greeted her in surprise as they met on the gallery landing, she fully dressed, he in a towelling robe and little else besides.

'Good morning.' Clare looked through him, unembarrassed.

'I've just woken Miles,' he relayed. 'We'll be down at eight o'clock.'

'Yes, sir.' Clare took it as an order. 'Do you prefer a cooked or continental breakfast?'

He frowned slightly before saying, 'Cooked, but nothing too heavy. Scrambled eggs will do, plus coffee and toast.'

'Very well, sir,' Clare responded, again with leaden politeness, and left him staring after her as she descended the staircase.

Obviously he hadn't expected her to know how to act the part of formal housekeeper, but she had a fair idea. She should do. She'd watched her mother present an inscrutable face to the Holsteads and their frequent rudeness. Now, in a similar position, she saw why. If she wanted to keep this job, being unobtrusive was probably as important as being efficient.

With her mind on being the latter, she searched for the kitchen. It was at the back of the house, a beautiful, fully modernised kitchen with built-in cupboards, cooker and every labour-saving gadget imaginable. Having not seen it on her first visit, Clare had feared a quaint, farmhouse sort, with impossible-to-keep-clean nooks and crannies and an impossible-to-cook-on range.

Her only problem was trying to fit into the overall she found hanging behind the larder door. Made of white cotton, it really did threaten to go round her twice. She had to dispense with the buttons and simply wrap herself in it and tie the belt very tightly. She ended up looking slightly ridiculous but that didn't bother her.

Breakfast was simple to prepare and was almost ready when the Marchands, father and son, trooped into the kitchen.

Clare, however, wasn't expecting them to sit down. 'I'm sorry. I've set the table in the dining-room.'

It was Miles who awarded her a critical look, before announcing, 'We never have breakfast *there*.'

'I'm sorry,' Clare repeated. 'If you give me a minute or two, I'll move everything back.'

'I should have told you,' Fen Marchand said, rising from the table. 'We'll move. Come on, Miles.'

The boy took his time in obeying and, before leaving the kitchen, he glanced smugly at her. Having fallen out of favour, Clare's mistakes were going to be tallied.

Not having time to worry about it, she concentrated on finishing the scrambled eggs and tipping them into a salver to keep warm. She'd already taken through two jugs of fruit juice and a first batch of tea and toast, and the Marchands were busy eating when she appeared. She served up the eggs, the man taking a fair portion, but leaving the same amount for the boy.

That didn't stop Miles from complaining, 'Is that all there is? I'm hungry.'

'I'll make more,' Clare said, resigned to the boy's rudeness.

But his father cut in, 'No, you won't. Miles, apologise!'

'What for?' the boy immediately protested.

'You know,' his father retorted. 'Either apologise or go to your room.'

The man clearly meant it. The boy's mouth went into a resentful line while his eyes flashed angrily in Clare's direction.

'*Apologise*!' his father insisted, a definite warning ring in his voice.

'Look, it doesn't matter.' Clare didn't want any pitch battles fought on her behalf, and, before Fen Marchand could make a bigger issue of it, she escaped to the kitchen.

She was preparing another batch of toast when Miles sidled into the room some five minutes later. He didn't speak but hung about at the door, his face a picture of sullenness.

He was a handsome boy, with the same blond hair and well-cut features as his father. He also had the Marchand eyes, a clear, penetrating blue that seemed so honest in Louise's case, and so chilling in the man's. On Miles, the eyes were windows of a troubled soul, following her as she moved about the kitchen.

'Can I get you something, Miles?' she eventually asked.

It gave him an opening and he blurted out, 'He says I have to apologise.'

Clare was unsurprised. 'Do you want to?'

'No,' the boy answered bluntly.

'Well, don't,' she told him just as bluntly, and, popping the toast into another rack, made for the door.

He stepped into her way. 'You'll tell him I haven't,' he said, more statement than question.

Clare shook her head. 'Why should I? You make enough trouble for yourself without any help from me.'

'It's him. He's on my case all the time,' Miles whined in complaint.

Perhaps it was true, but Clare wasn't about to take sides. She didn't want to end up playing piggy-in-the-middle.

'That's your problem, Miles,' she said, more roughly than she intended.

He actually looked hurt for a second, before getting his own back. 'My dad was right. You're not a good influence on me at all,' he had the nerve to declare.

Clare's brows rose. 'He said that to you?'

'Yes...sort of.' The boy's manner became cagey, as if he wasn't quite telling the truth.

She guessed, 'To your aunt?'

He nodded. 'I overheard them. After I got rid of the last woman, Aunt Lou persuaded him to give you a try. He didn't want to, though.'

It was hardly news to Clare and she shrugged it off, asking instead, 'Do they know you listen at doors for a hobby?'

He hunched his shoulders. 'Why? Are you going to tell them?'

'We seem to have come full circle,' she pointed out. 'Why don't we have an agreement? You don't get in my way and I won't get in yours. Now...' She waited patiently for him to move himself from the door.

He did so reluctantly, not sure how to counteract.

Clare left him still deciding as she went through to the dining-room with the toast-rack in her hand. The man had his head stuck in a newspaper and she hoped she might get away with just dumping the rack and disappearing.

No such luck, as he looked up to ask, 'Did Miles come to see you?'

'Yes,' she confirmed, then busied herself stacking some of the dirty plates on a tray.

'And?' He took off his glasses and fixed her with those chilly blue eyes.

'He said you wanted him to apologise,' she replied truthfully, 'although it really wasn't necessary.'

'I think I should be the judge of that,' he firmly put her in her place, before continuing, 'Still, if he's apologised, then I'm prepared to let the matter drop there.'

Pompous ass, Clare thought as she trotted out a meek, 'Yes, sir,' and a suitably servile, 'Will that be all, sir?'

'Yes. No.' He squinted at her in disapproval. 'What are you wearing?'

'An overall...sir,' she answered with visible restraint.

'Yes, well, it doesn't exactly fit, does it?' he pointed out the obvious. 'You look like a washerwoman.'

This time what Clare thought wasn't printable. She wondered if he went out of his way to be rude or if he achieved it without effort.

'Here.' He produced his wallet and drew out thirty pounds. 'Get something more presentable to wear.'

Clare had no choice but to take the money, asking, 'What do you suggest, sir?'

'I don't know.' He scowled at her. 'Anything, as long as it fits.'

'Very well, sir.' Clare made to go.

He burst out in bad temper, 'And you can stop that, too!'

'Sir?' She turned questioning eyes in his direction.

'Yes, sir, no, sir, three bags full, sir,' he threw back at her, his lips curling in distaste. 'The Uriah Heep act might go down well with your average prison warder, but I find it repellent ... So, do you think you could manage politeness without servility, Miss...?' He waved a hand, having forgotten her name again.

'Anderson,' Clare supplied, before adding in grudging tones, 'I'll try.'

'Do!' he instructed, and had the final word as he stuck his head back in his newspaper.

Clare seethed her way out of the room. Obviously she was the only one obliged to be polite.

She returned to the kitchen to find Miles now sitting at the table with a bowl of cereal and a comic.

He slid her an accusing look. 'I bet you told him.'

'How much?' she countered.

He frowned. 'How much what?'

'How much do you bet?' she repeated. 'A weeks' pocket money? Two weeks'?'

'You mean you didn't tell him,' he concluded, still in suspicious tones.

Clare shook her head. 'He assumed you'd apologised. I didn't disillusion him,' she said, a shrug dismissing the subject.

But the boy actually came back with a murmur of, 'Thanks.'

She acknowledged it with a brief smile, before turning her attention to the dishes. There was a dishwasher, which made things relatively easy—or would have done if she'd ever operated one before.

She was standing puzzling over the machine's controls when Miles appeared at her side.

'It's simple,' he claimed, every inch the superior male. 'You just put the powder and rinse in the dispensers, check the salt level, and turn the control to wash.'

Clare frowned. 'How do you check the salt level?'

'See the cap there, under the tray? If green is showing, you don't need salt,' he explained.

Clare continued to frown. 'I don't see any green.'

'Well, that's because it does need salt,' he declared, patient in the face of her slowness.

'I see.' She nodded, and, walking over to a cupboard, came back with a jar of cooking salt.

This amused the boy greatly. 'Not that kind of salt. Don't you know anything?' he asked in pitying tones.

'It seems not,' Clare conceded. 'Perhaps you'd like to return the favour and show me.'

'OK,' he agreed easily, and, going into the cupboard below the sink, appeared with a bag of special salt. He unscrewed the cap, poured a good measure of salt in, and screwed it on again, all the while telling her, 'Three housekeepers ago hadn't the first idea either. I told her you had to pack sand into it and I got her some from the garden. Would you believe she actually used it?' he said with a gleeful laugh.

'Maybe she was crazy enough to trust you,' Clare suggested drily, wondering if he was also leading her up the garden path.

'It's OK,' the boy understood, 'I'm doing it right for you. Like you said, favour for a favour.'

'That's a relief.' Clare's lips quirked into a half-smile as she went on to ask, 'So, what happened with the sand?'

'Oh, nothing much,' he dismissed airily. 'The machine broke down, of course, and we had to get a plumber in, but old Horseface was too embarrassed to tell Dad she'd put sand in the machine.'

'Old Horseface,' Clare repeated with raised eyebrows. 'That's not a very nice thing to call someone.'

'Well, *she* wasn't very nice,' he claimed in defensive tones. 'You should have heard some of the things she called me when she was loaded.'

'Loaded?' Clare echoed.

'Drunk,' he explained quite casually. 'She used to drink all the time.'

Clare looked sceptical. She had a feeling Miles Marchand had only a nodding acquaintance with the truth.

But he insisted, 'She *did*!' and, taking hold of Clare's arm, drew her towards the pantry-room. 'She kept a bottle here. Inside one of the stone jars on the top shelf. I bet it's still there.'

He pointed towards the shelf he meant and, positioning stool steps underneath, motioned for Clare to go up and check.

She did so reluctantly, wondering if some trick was being played on her. The first jar proved empty, the second one full of lentils. She showed it to Miles, but he insisted she try the next.

Sure enough, the third jar clinked as Clare lifted it from the shelf and, putting in her hand, she drew out a bottle of gin with a small measure left inside.

She was holding it in her hand and congratulating Miles on his observation, when a dry cough made her aware that they had an audience. At some time Fenwick Marchand had appeared in the doorway.

He looked from one to another, then at the gin bottle, before saying, 'Isn't it a bit early for a party?'

'I...we...it's not how it looks,' Clare volunteered rather lamely, while Miles piped up, 'No, I can explain.'

'That won't be necessary, Miles,' his father answered in a surprisingly calm tone, before switching to ask, 'Are you ready? I thought we'd go into Oxford now.'

'I...I have to get my pocket money.' The boy looked relieved at the change of subject.

'Then I'll meet you at the car.' The man shifted away from the door to allow him to pass.

The boy escaped gratefully. Clare didn't blame him. She wished she could do the same. Instead she continued to stand on the little step-ladder, holding the evidence.

'I know what you must be thinking,' she said as the man turned back to fix his cold blue eyes on her, 'but this doesn't belong to me.'

'Don't tell me. You just happened to come across it,' he suggested, raising a brow.

'In a sense, yes,' Clare agreed. 'You see, I was looking for some—er—split peas...and Miles thought they might be here, and instead we found this bottle of—um—gin. God knows how it got there.'

'But it's not yours,' he concluded for her in a surprisingly mild tone.

She shook her head. 'As I told you, I don't drink. And even if I did, I don't like gin... Though I don't suppose you believe me,' she finished, more resigned than angry.

'As a matter of fact,' he responded concisely, 'I do.'

'You *do*?' Clare wondered if she'd heard right.

'I do,' he confirmed.

'But why?' Clare would have convicted herself on the evidence.

'Our last housekeeper but two had a fondness for peppermints,' he explained. 'That usually means one of two things: either the person likes the taste of peppermint or likes the taste of something else. I sacked her when I discovered which. Presumably Miles was just showing you where she hid her drink supply,' he announced in Sherlock Holmes style.

Clare was visibly relieved. She'd thought he'd send her packing, bottle in hand.

He seemed to read her mind as he went on, 'I operate on the principle of innocent until proven guilty, Miss... True, I have some doubts about your suitability for this post, but I will not be looking for an excuse to sack you. Is that understood?'

'Yes, si—Mr Marchand.'

'Good.' He nodded, and, turning on his heel, departed.

Clare sat down on the top of the step-ladder and let out the breath she'd been holding. She really had believed her number was up. Instead she was left wondering if she'd misjudged Fen Marchand.

She considered the possibility for a moment, before shaking her head at the idea. Fair he might be, but she still suspected that under that grim exterior lay an equally grim interior.

A month later and nothing had changed Clare's opinion. He spoke to her only when necessary. His 'Good morning's and his 'Goodnight's were perfunctory, mere conventional politeness. Between breakfast and dinner, they had virtually no contact.

It was the boy Clare saw most of. When he wasn't out with his father, he hung around the kitchen, bored and restless, some days pleasant, other days sullen and difficult. Whichever, Clare remained detached. It was obvious that he craved attention and affection, but she wasn't able to give either. And what good would it have done, forming any kind of attachment, when she was just passing through his life?

In fact, she still expected Fenwick Marchand to announce any day that he was dispensing with her services.

A Mrs Hailey from Domestics Ltd had telephoned a couple of times when he was out, declining to leave a message. It was fairly obvious that he intended to find a replacement for her, irrespective of how hard she worked in the house or how well she cooked for them.

That was why she felt no real surprise when one day, after breakfast, he asked her to step into his study. She was resigned. She wasn't going to make a fuss when he sacked her.

'Please sit down.' He waved her into the chair on the opposite side of the desk.

She sat and waited.

He took his time, plainly uncomfortable as he shuffled the papers around his desk. He cleared his throat before finally beginning, 'You are probably aware that the agreed trial period for your employment has expired.'

'Yes, it's all right.' Clare took pity on him. 'If you could just give me a week to make alternate arrangements—and I'd be grateful for a reference, too.'

'Reference?' he repeated, as if such a thing had never occurred to him.

'I don't expect you to lie about my past,' she pursued hastily. 'However, you could say I work quite hard—assuming you think so,' she added.

His brows drew together above his heavy-framed spectacles. 'You're prepared to leave, just like that?'

What did he expect? Tears?

'There's not much point in arguing, is there?' she shrugged. 'If you've made up your mind, you're not going to change it.'

'I think we may be talking at cross purposes, Miss...' Once again he searched for her surname; he'd probably never considered it worth committing to memory.

'Anderson,' Clare supplied with a little irritation, 'and I don't think so. I'm a realist. I always knew you'd look for someone else. When does she start?'

'Who?' He feigned perplexity rather well.

But Clare had no doubts. 'The new housekeeper from the agency.'

He shook his head. 'Let's get this straight. You believe I've employed another housekeeper behind your back?'

'If that's the way you want to put it.' Pride made her seem indifferent.

His face darkened with anger, reminding her of the one time he'd lost his temper with her, outside Oxford Station. She was glad the space of a desk separated them.

'I realise, Miss...Miss Anderson that you may be used to such behaviour from the men with whom you normally associate,' he spoke with chilling contempt. 'I, however, operate by a different code of ethics. I said I'd give you a trial and I have. I have not, in the interim, sought a replacement.'

'Oh yes?' Clare challenged rather recklessly. 'So what about that Mrs Hailey? Domestics Ltd? I suppose she just rang to talk about the weather.'

'Why Mrs Hailey rang me is not really any of your business,' she was informed in cutting tones. 'Nevertheless, you may as well know that she *had* found me a possible housekeeper, being under the impression I was still looking for one. I explained the post had been filled but would re-contact her should it fall vacant once more.'

'Oh.' This time the monosyllable was an embarrassed murmur from Clare.

'In point of fact,' he continued, grim-faced, 'I am satisfied with the standard of your work and had intended to offer you the appointment on a permanent basis. Unfortunately, the apparent ease with which you're prepared to leave my employ has given me cause to reconsider my decision,' he announced on a steely note.

Clare's heart sank as she realised what she'd just done—talked herself out of a job.

'When you asked to speak to me,' she tried to excuse herself, 'I thought...well, I thought that was it. I mean, you never said you were happy with my work. I assumed——'

'Too much, it seems,' he cut in abruptly, then continued at his pompous worst, 'If I may offer some advice, Miss Anderson, regarding future employers, I would recommend you adopt a more…conciliatory approach.'

'What do you mean?' Clare responded in a less than conciliatory manner. 'I've done my best to fit in. I've cooked your meals, cleaned your house, and otherwise kept out of your way. That's what you wanted, wasn't it?' she challenged.

'Yes,' he granted, his lips thinning in irritation, 'but do you have to make it quite so obvious that you resent every minute spent here?'

'I don't,' Clare denied automatically, not having really analysed her feelings.

'Don't you?' His blue eyes were sceptical behind the heavy-framed glasses. 'Then why do I get the impression you would sooner be back in prison sewing mailbags?' he enquired with dark humour.

'We don't do that any more,' she stated, her own face a picture of the resentment to which he'd alluded.

'No, of course,' he drawled back, 'it's all therapy sessions and Open University degrees these days.'

His remark did nothing to improve Clare's temper. It was true she'd had the chance to study in prison and had, in fact, gained three A levels. But that hadn't made up for the bad food, the claustrophobic cells or the basic loss of liberty. It hadn't cured the boredom or given her any protection against the more violent of the women prisoners. And, in the end, it hadn't done anything for her prospects of a job. An ex-con with A levels was still an ex-con.

'You're right. It was almost a holiday camp,' she said with biting sarcasm as she abandoned all hope of retaining her job. 'You can't imagine the fun I had. All girls together, such pleasant company, quite fascinating lives, some of them had. I learned masses of interesting

stuff about shop-lifting and drug-pedalling and prostitution. You wouldn't credit how——'

'All right, you've made your point,' he cut in
brusquely. 'So prison doesn't do much in the way of
character-building. But that still doesn't alter the issue.
If you want to get a job and keep it, you're going to
have to improve your attitude,' he advised in paternal-
istic tones.

Pompous ass, Clare thought, not for the first time,
but, seeing no purpose in arguing, didn't. Instead she
muttered a perfunctory, 'Yes, fine,' and, getting to her
feet, asked point-blank, 'Will you give me a reference
or not?'

He didn't even take time to think about it, answering
in the same vein, 'Not.'

'OK, I won't beg,' she threw at him, and, with a last
look that didn't hide her dislike, walked towards the
door.

He got there just behind her, crossing the study and
closing the door on her before she'd even properly
opened it.

She rounded on him in anger and he caught her by
the arms, preventing any possibility of her slapping him.
He hadn't forgotten the incident at the station, either.

'Let me go!' she spat at him, only to have his grip
tighten. She winced a little in pain as his fingers bit into
the flesh of her forearms, bare beneath the short sleeves
of her new overall.

'Go and do what?' he challenged. 'You don't seem to
realise I'm your only chance and you've just done your
best to blow it.'

'Don't flatter yourself! I can manage well enough
without you and your job,' she claimed wildly.

'Really?' He lifted a derisive brow. 'So how? Tell me.
Without a reference and with a record.'

'I . . . It's none of your business!' Stuck for an answer,
she tried and failed to twist free.

He pushed her against the door. 'I'll tell you how. You're not going to manage. You're going to carry on slamming the door on anyone who tries to help you, until you find one day there are no doors left to slam! Then you're going to find yourself on the street, selling the only thing you have left—your body!'

'That's rubbish!' Clare denied furiously. 'I'd never do that. I'd die first.'

'You *think* you would,' he went on insidiously, 'but the human instinct is geared for survival. You'd die inside all right, every time some man took his pleasure with you. And you'd be stripped of that terrible, fierce pride of yours. But you'd still go on, eating and sleeping, getting through the day.'

He sounded so certain, it was as if he had the power to look into her future: absurd! He knew nothing of her or her life. He lived a cloistered existence, a million miles from her world. If he knew anything about prostitution and the like, it probably came from reading an article in a newspaper.

Yet he was so articulate on the subject, it reduced Clare to a helpless silence. He wasn't right. He couldn't be. She wasn't like that. But the very idea turned indignation to dread. For what was she going to do, when she walked out of his door?

'Listen to me.' He spoke more gently as he saw the colour drain from her face. 'You don't have to leave like this. When I said I wasn't going to give you a reference, it was because I have no intention of sacking you.'

'But...I don't understand.' Clare raised confused eyes to his face. Hadn't he already sacked her?

'I want you to stay,' he said in very clear terms.

Still she shook her head. 'You can't. Why should you? My attitude——'

'Stinks,' he stated with brutal frankness. 'However, your cooking doesn't. Nor does your cleaning. And you're the first housekeeper I've had who's been able to tolerate Miles. So, the truth is, we need each other.'

'I don't——' Clare began to deny any need on her side, then caught herself up, before her pride got her into more trouble. Instead, she admitted grudgingly, 'The job suits me well enough, so I'm prepared to stay.'

'Good.' He nodded in approval, then, realising he was still holding her, dropped his arms to his sides. His grip had been quite hard and the marks of his fingers were clearly visible on her skin. 'I'm sorry. I didn't mean to hurt you,' he added, frowning over the fact.

'It's all right.' Clare was too tough to worry over such a minor injury.

But he continued to frown, his eyes shifting from her arms to her face as he said, 'You're very thin. Do you eat properly?'

'What?' The question threw Clare.

'I've never seen you eat,' he pursued in almost suspicious tones. 'You're not anorexic, are you?'

'No, of course not,' she declared at this less than flattering suggestion. 'I just don't have a large appetite.'

'Hmm.' He didn't look particularly impressed by her explanation, and reluctantly concluded, 'Perhaps you should eat with us... Yes, that would be best.'

Clare was appalled at the idea. She didn't want to eat *en famille*, especially after such a graceless invitation. 'There's no need,' she said quickly.

'Nevertheless, I'd prefer it.' He reverted to his more usual autocratic manner.

Clare didn't have the energy to argue with him. She let him think her silence was an improvement of 'attitude'.

'Dinner.' He nodded at his own pronouncement, then looked rather pained at the decision he'd made.

'All right.' Clare took it as a dismissal and quickly slipped out of the door.

She returned to the kitchen to find Miles still there, reading a comic over the mess of breakfast. She must have looked as nerve-racked as she felt, for he asked, 'What's wrong?'

She shook her head. 'Nothing.'

'Yes, there is,' he pursued. 'You look really upset. He hasn't sacked you, has he?'

'No,' she said, hardly able to believe it herself. 'If you must know, I've been given the job on a permanent basis.'

The boy smiled fleetingly before pulling a face, as if the news displeased him. Clare didn't take his reaction too much to heart. Miles pulled a face at most things.

'No wonder you look sick,' he eventually commented. 'I bet you were hoping for a month's money and a one-way ticket out of this hell-hole.'

Clare raised a reproving brow at this profanity, but otherwise said nothing. She hoped that one day Miles would tire of trying to shock her; so far, she hoped in vain.

'Never mind, you're bound to get lucky soon,' he added but with a grin that was more cheeky than malicious.

'Get lucky?' was echoed by Fen Marchand as he walked into the kitchen. 'Lucky in what?' His eyes went from Miles to Clare, expecting an answer.

They both said simultaneously, 'Nothing,' like a pair of thieves caught in the act, then Miles did a runner, saying,

'Got to find my riding hat.'

He escaped and left Clare on the spot with his father. 'Decidedly conspiratorial,' Fen Marchand commented drily.

'What?' Clare said rather stupidly.

'You and my son,' he explained. 'Whenever I enter a room, I feel I've just missed something.'

'I don't know what you mean.' Clare feigned ignorance.

'You surprise me. I had thought you quite intelligent,' he countered with heavy irony.

Clare gritted her teeth. No one had ever exasperated her the way this man did.

'Lucky in love, perhaps?' he went on to suggest.

Clare stared at him dumbly. It took her a moment to realise they'd gone two steps back in the conversation. When she did, she responded leadenly, 'Do you really imagine I'd want to discuss my love life with an eleven-year-old?'

'No,' he conceded, 'but that wouldn't stop Miles. As you may have gathered, my son has a very doubtful interest in the affairs of adults. His mother saw to that.'

The last was said with an anger so controlled that it made Clare shiver. He showed so little emotion most of the time that she believed he felt none. Yet there were moments, like this one, when she sensed that a very different person lived behind that expressionless mask.

He had loved his wife and now he hated her. It was that simple. Or was it?

'At any rate, I'd be grateful if you don't encourage his...precociousness,' he stated politely enough.

Clare still resented it. 'Don't worry! I know my place!'

'Your place?' he echoed, brows lifting, before he interpreted, 'Being just a humble servant, you mean?'

Clare's face was stony. 'If you like.'

He gave a short laugh. 'My dear Miss...' As usual he'd forgotten her surname and didn't try very hard to remember. '"Humble" has to be the absolutely last word I'd ever use to describe you.'

Offended, Clare glared openly at him. It proved his point. His mouth slanted, amused, mocking, then, having had the final say, he turned on his heel and departed.

Clare was left clenching her fists and asking herself how long she could stand working for such a man. She pictured herself walking out, here and now, and leaving the Marchands to fend for themselves. That would wipe the smile off his face for a day or two. So what was stopping her?

She recalled her earlier encounter with Fenwick and the things he'd said. Working for him was her best chance. Who else would have her, with a record and no reference? And where else could she go, but the streets?

Was he right? She shook her head in fierce denial but couldn't come up with any alternatives. Walk out on this job and she instantly became homeless.

Clare decided she must stop kidding herself and start facing reality. At the moment this job kept her from the streets, and her pride was a luxury she couldn't afford. It might be galling to admit, and difficult to accept, but the truth was she needed Fenwick Marchand a great deal more than he needed her.

CHAPTER FOUR

HAVING accepted her own vulnerability made it no easier for Clare to like Fenwick Marchand, and she was relieved when he took Miles to a riding school for the day.

She spent the morning cleaning the house, made herself a quick sandwich, then went up to her room to spend the afternoon reading, as usual. She was just considering returning downstairs to prepare dinner when there was a slight knock on the door.

'Yes?' She guessed it might be Miles.

It was—a Miles looking the happiest she'd ever seen him.

'Come in,' she invited as he hesitated in the doorway.

He didn't need a second asking and, grinning broadly, crossed the room to bounce down on the bed.

'How was it?' she smiled.

'Absolutely fantastic!' he declared loudly. 'I thought it might be boring, like lessons or something. But it wasn't. You should have seen the horses. And the jumps! Wow!' He motioned with his hands to illustrate the height of the fences he'd jumped.

Clare suspected he was exaggerating, but it gave her pleasure to see him so happy. Gone was the moody morose child that mooched round the house most days. In his place was a typical eleven-year-old, full of energy and enthusiasm, and without a care in the world.

Clare listened as he gave an account of his day. Apparently horse-riding had been followed by a pizza in town and the purchase of a new pair of trainers. She noticed that 'Dad says' prefixed many of his sentences. She also noticed a difference in his accent; he sounded more English than American. It wasn't the first time she'd wondered if his transatlantic drawl was deliberately put on. After all, how long had he spent in L.A.— a matter of months, according to Louise?

'The instructor says I could be a really good rider.' He returned to the high point of his day. 'It's just that I haven't had enough practice yet.'

'I thought you had a horse when you lived with your grandfather.' Clare frowned.

'I did,' he nodded, 'but my grandfather was always too busy to take me to the stables... Still, at least *he* wanted me,' the boy concluded fiercely.

Clare could have left it and tried to lighten the mood again. After all, Fen Marchand had made it clear that he wouldn't welcome her interference. Yet for some reason she couldn't let it pass.

'Your father wanted you, too.' She stated what his aunt Lou had told her.

But Miles shook his head. 'No, he didn't,' he claimed, angry now, with her, his father, the world. 'He knew I hated it in London, but he wouldn't take me home.'

It was that simple to the boy, and a warning voice in Clare's head said, Leave the matter alone, but the unfairness of it wouldn't let her.

'Things aren't always so straightforward, Miles.' She chose her words carefully. 'Your father wanted you to carry on living with him, but your mother and grandfather wanted you too, so in the end a judge had to decide... You know what a judge is?' she asked and it drew a nod. 'Well, your dad had to accept his decision. Otherwise he might have been put in gaol.'

Miles stared at her, round-eyed. It was obviously all news to him. Clare wondered if she'd made one big mistake, telling him. She didn't want to damage him further.

Then Miles asked, 'Is that true? They made Dad give me up?'

'Well, a judge did.' Clare didn't feel he should transfer his resentment wholesale from his father to his mother and grandfather. 'Everybody wanted you, so someone had to decide.'

'Why did no one ask me?' Miles tried to make sense of it—these adult arrangements.

'I don't know,' Clare admitted. 'I suppose because you were only eight.'

'Huh!' It was a sound of disgust from a boy who knew his mind now and probably had at eight, too. 'Grown-ups think they know everything, but they really know nothing... Except for you, Clare. You're special,' he concluded.

Clare smiled, then shook her head. 'No, I'm not. I'm just a housekeeper,' she reminded him and herself, and, glancing at her watch, added, 'A very late housekeeper.'

So saying, she put on her overall, washed her face at the basin and passed a quick brush through her hair, now grown into a bob covering her ears.

Miles watched her in silence, but said as they went downstairs together, 'Don't you ever wear make-up?'

Clare shook her head. She'd never worn much make-up even before prison and she'd got out of the habit there.

'My mother used to plaster it on.' Miles grimaced.

'Well...' Clare searched for something positive to say '...it was probably worth the bother in your mother's case. I bet she was a very beautiful lady.'

He shrugged. 'I suppose.'

The boy obviously had few good memories of his mother, but perhaps it was hardly surprising.

He walked with her downstairs, then disappeared to his hut in the woods, while Clare took herself through to the kitchen.

She prepared a Hungarian goulash for dinner—a dish she could cook in her sleep—and spent the time mulling over the day's events. She supposed it was a good day in that she'd been given the housekeeping job on a permanent basis, but, instead of feeling satisfaction, she was left with a feeling of deep disquiet over the boy and his future.

Clare's mind switched involuntarily to her own past. She, too, had felt unloved as a child, but then she probably had been. She pictured herself at seventeen, scared, pregnant. And her mother, practical, relentless. Clare had gone to her for help, and Mary Anderson had listened in resigned, unsurprised silence, before saying, 'You've been stupid, but I'll take care of it.'

Her tone had scarcely been sympathetic but Clare had felt relief. Everything was going to be all right. Her mother would take care of her.

It was two days later before Clare had realised exactly what her mother had said. It was only when she'd handed her a few hundred pounds and the name and address of a clinic that Clare had understood that *it*, not she, was to be taken care of.

She'd cried the whole night, packed her bag the next day, taken the money and thrown away the address.

She'd kept in touch with her mother, sending her a photograph of Peter at birth, but there had been no invitation to return home. Not until her mother had been in the last stages of cancer and had decided she didn't want to die alone. Even then, she'd taken little notice of Peter, the grandson she would rather not have had.

'I can pay back some of the money now,' Clare had offered, referring to the few hundred with which she'd left home.

Her mother had shaken her head. 'You didn't imagine that was mine, did you, girl?'

'So, where did you get it?' Clare asked, still naïve.

Her mother smiled, a small, bitter smile. 'From someone who wanted a grandchild even less than I did.'

It took Clare just a moment to work out. 'Him or her?'

'His lordship,' Mary Anderson admitted. 'She's a Catholic, or was.'

Clare caught on more quickly this time. Her mother had avoided Lady Abbotsford because she'd been uncertain whether religious conscience would have allowed her to foot the bill.

'What about Johnny? Does he know?' Clare asked, and accepted her mother's terse denial.

She met Johnny, her second day back. She was walking from the village shop, when he passed her in his sports car. He recognised her in his mirror and braked, waiting for her to catch up.

'Long time no see,' he said in greeting while his eyes roamed over her, searching for changes. He saw none for he added, 'Still as beautiful as ever, Red.'

Her heart lurched for an instant at the nickname, then she snapped back, 'Don't call me that!'

'Why not?' He smiled his dark, dangerous smile. 'You don't think I've forgotten, do you?'

He held her eyes, and she felt his overpowering attraction once more. She prayed for sanity, and instead found herself accepting his offer of a lift.

Four-year-old Peter was where she'd left him, digging holes in the front garden of her mother's cottage. The gate was locked and her mother was watching him from the porchway.

'Whose is the sprog?' Johnny frowned.

'Mine,' Clare admitted shortly.

'And there was me, believing you'd remain faithful.' He feigned broken-heartedness.

She recovered her sanity and muttered, 'Why? You didn't.'

'Technically, no,' he conceded, 'I could hardly refuse to do my conjugal duty, even if it meant shutting my eyes and thinking of England.'

Clare laughed. He'd always been able to make her laugh. But now, thankfully, she saw right through his charming lies.

'I wonder—does the Lady Elizabeth know how you suffer?' she asked, tongue-in-cheek.

He shrugged. 'I shouldn't think so. Liz spends too much time of her time on the ski slopes to notice. In fact, we've come to an agreement. As the skiing's pretty well non-existent in Buckinghamshire and the nightlife's somewhat limited in Klosters, we've accepted the hardship of quite lengthy separations.'

'Really?' Clare wasn't sure whether to believe him or not, but it mattered little to her. 'People have just no idea how the upper classes suffer,' she said with heavy irony, before climbing out of his car.

He called after her, 'You've grown harder, Red.'

And she called back, 'Believe it.'

He didn't, of course, and every second day brought a telephone call. Clare found herself able to resist his persuasiveness, but dreaded the complications of his discovering that Peter was his son.

Her mother died some weeks later. She'd been in great pain and her release had been welcome. She was buried next to the husband who had died more than twenty years earlier.

The Holstead family came *en masse* to the funeral. His lordship cut Clare dead, of course, but Lady Abbotsford uttered a few words of consolation, as well as insisting that Clare treat the estate cottage as her own until she had somewhere else to go.

Sarah, Johnny's sister, was the kindest. She'd married a barrister and lived in the next county. She mentioned their nursery days with Clare's mother, and, in doing so, reminded Clare of a time when her mother had seemed a kinder, gentler person. It had been working half a lifetime for the Holsteads that had soured her.

Afterwards Clare hadn't intended to stay long in her mother's cottage, but finding alternative accommodation proved difficult. In Brighton she'd shared a flat with another single mum and worked nights as a hotel receptionist, but she'd had to give up both job and room to return home to nurse her mother, and, with her mother dying in early December, it wasn't the best time to search for new work.

In the end she remained at the cottage for Christmas and that was when Johnny started to come round. She tried to discourage him, but he took little notice. Perhaps she didn't try very hard: she was lonely and his visits brightened her life and Peter's.

Of course he wanted to sleep with her, but she resisted. She was no longer seventeen and stupid. She knew, whether she went to bed with him or not, that he'd eventually tire of playing at Happy Families with Peter and her.

She was right. In February he disappeared back to London, and she didn't see him again till the spring.

She was still at the cottage, but by then her life had begun to fall apart. Peter was sick, some rare blood disorder, his only chance treatment in America. She'd already gone, cap in hand, to Lord Abbotsford, and he'd turned her away, refusing to pay for a grandson he'd never acknowledged. So, when Johnny returned for Easter, she approached him.

She told him straight. Peter was his son. His son was dying. Money was needed.

Johnny looked sick himself, his face almost haggard and his nerves on edge. At first Clare expected him to deny fatherhood, but he didn't. He just sat down, put his head in his hands and rambled on about the mess he'd made of his life.

Clare felt no sympathy. All her love was focused on Peter. She repeated the sum she needed—thirty thousand pounds—loose change to the Holsteads.

When Johnny claimed not to have the money, she spat on him. Physically spat on him. A disgusting thing to do, yet Johnny scarcely reacted.

A fortnight passed before she saw him again. This time he was excitable and nervous. He said he was willing to help, but only if she helped him. He was going to raise the cash by selling one of the racers in the Holstead stables. She was to accompany him and the horse, and collect the money from the buyer. They would then travel on to London where she would act as messenger for Johnny, paying off a gambling debt for him. She would then get her share of the money.

It seemed an unnecessarily elaborate plan but Peter's plight consumed her and she went along with it. It was only much later that she wondered how she could have been so naïve.

She thought now of the events that had followed and a tear sprang to her eye. She brushed it away, then jumped a little as she turned and saw Fenwick Marchand standing at the door.

'What's wrong?' His eyes narrowed on her.

'Wrong?' she echoed, while she mentally dragged herself back from the past. 'I...why should anything be wrong?'

'You tell me,' he invited, aware that she was on the verge of tears.

She shook her head and said, 'Nothing, I was just peeling onions.'

'Really?' He looked at the object in her hand and pointed out, 'I'm not much of a cook, but that looks more like a potato to me.'

The sarcasm helped Clare to recover her composure. If she ever felt tempted to cry on anyone's shoulder, it certainly wouldn't be Fenwick Marchand's.

'Earlier—I was peeling them earlier.' She looked at him stonily, discouraging any further probing.

He shrugged, and switched to asking, 'Do you know where Miles is?'

'In his hut, I think,' she replied, then went on hesitantly, 'Listen, I—um——'

'Yes?' He waited for her to continue.

Clare felt she should tell him about her discussion with Miles concerning custody, but she feared his reaction. He might regard it as interference in his personal life

and he'd probably be right. She had overstepped the
mark between servant and master.

'Nothing. It's not important.' She clammed up again.

He stood for a moment, watching her. 'Look, if
something's worrying you, please feel free to say. I realise you are very...isolated, living here.'

'I don't mind,' Clare insisted, her face expressionless.

He frowned, as if he didn't want to leave things there,
then gave a sigh of dismissal, before saying, 'Very well,
I'll see you at dinner.'

It reminded Clare that earlier, in what was turning out
to be a very long day, he'd suggested she start eating *en
famille*. She didn't want to, of course, and, hoping he'd
forgotten, set only two places in the dining-room.

He hadn't. When she served the meat and laid the
vegetables on the table for them to help themselves, he
said, 'You may recall that I suggested you dine with us.'

'I...' Clare searched for an excuse, but then caught
Miles's eye appealing for her to agree.

'Fetch an extra serving,' Marchand added insistently.

Clare might have argued, but she was just too tired.
She seemed to have spent the day picking her way
through an emotional minefield. Surely she could survive
one dinner. Tomorrow, she would come up with an
excuse.

She went through to get a plate, and came back to
find an extra place set opposite Miles. The boy smiled
broadly at her.

She sat down and did her very best to become invisible.

At first it seemed to work. Still in good spirits, Miles
talked with his father about their afternoon at the riding
school. She was surprised to find Fen Marchand quite
knowledgeable about horses. Although there was a small
block of stables at the back of Woodside Hall, it was
unoccupied and so spick and span, it suggested no horses
had lived there for a long time.

'This must be boring for you.' Fen Marchand suddenly included her in the conversation.

'Pardon?' Clare hadn't expected any such consideration.

'All this talk of horses,' he added at her vacant look.

'No, I—um—don't mind,' she answered quite truthfully.

And Miles supplied for her, 'Clare used to ride when she was young. She cleaned out these people's stables and they let her ride their horses in return.'

'Really?' Fen Marchand looked surprised. 'I had you down as a city person. Where was this?'

'Buckinghamshire,' Clare admitted reluctantly.

'Where's that?' Miles asked.

'You'd know if you'd studied that map of the UK I gave you,' his father said drily.

Clare answered vaguely, 'North of London.'

'The next county to ours, actually,' Fen remarked, enquiring of her, 'Where exactly?'

'South Buckinghamshire.' It was hardly an exact description and his eyes revealed that he'd noted the fact.

But he did not pursue it, saying instead, 'In that case, should you wish to visit your family, I could lend you a car.'

Clare didn't hide her surprise. She asked, tongue-in-cheek, 'Your Jag?'

He smiled a little, realising she was joking. 'There's a VW Golf in one of the garages. I keep it for emergencies and use by any housekeepers without their own transport . . . I meant to say.'

Clare just bet he did! She'd already been there a month and he'd not so much as mentioned the said car. The reason was fairly obvious. He hadn't trusted her not to disappear with it.

Clare supposed it was understandable. After all, why should he trust someone he already knew to be a thief?

Their eyes met across the table and Clare returned his stare for a moment, wondering if he really trusted her now. Or was it some kind of test? A slight smile played on his lips, but its meaning eluded her. His steady blue gaze told her nothing, and she was the first to look away, suddenly conscious of the intimacy of their eye contact.

'So, would you like use of it?' he prompted at her silence.

'Go on,' Miles encouraged. 'If you had a car, you could take me swimming.'

'Don't put her off.' The dry comment came from his father, but his smile made it a joke and Miles pulled a face in return.

'Sorry,' Clare addressed the boy, 'but I'm afraid I haven't a licence.'

'You can't drive?' the man concluded in almost shocked tones.

That wasn't quite what Clare had said, but she didn't correct him. Instead she replied a little sharply, 'It's not a crime, is it?'

'Well, no...of course not.' His tone was now surprisingly conciliatory. 'It's just that most young people seem to learn these days.'

'Young people'? Was that how he saw her? Clare wished she still felt young.

'I was busy learning other things.' Clare meant more basic things—like how to earn a living and raise a child— but as soon as her words were out she realised how they might be interpreted.

Fen stared at her again, this time with no trace of a smile.

It was Miles who said, 'What things?' with overt curiosity.

Just for an instant Clare was tempted to say, Safecracking, or, maybe, House burglary. It was what his father was thinking.

But the man beat her to it, saying for Miles's benefit, 'Clare means she was at college, studying Domestic Science. Isn't that correct?' He willed her to agree and not to reveal her true past.

It was Miles who contradicted him, 'No, she doesn't. Clare's never been to college. She told me so.'

'Really?' The man's eyes remained on Clare, accusing her of a catalogue of unspecified sins. 'It seems, Miss Anderson, that you've been more forthcoming with my son than myself——'

'Clare,' Miles directed at his father.

'What?' His father's eyes switched back to him.

'Clare. You called her that earlier,' the boy pointed out. 'Miss Anderson sounds very...' Miles paused to find the correct word.

Clare assumed 'pompous' wasn't included in his vocabulary as yet.

'Yes, possibly,' his father agreed impatiently, before directing at her, 'Anyway, *Clare*, it would be useful for all concerned if you could drive. I'll arrange lessons.'

Just like that, Clare thought, as he failed to consult her.

'I can't afford lessons,' she stated bluntly, ignoring the fact that she'd just been paid. She was saving every penny for the day when her services would no longer be required.

He made a dismissive gesture. 'I'll pay, of course.'

'No, thank you,' Clare said with leaden politeness, and rose quickly to collect the plates.

She hoped the subject would be forgotten by the time she brought dessert. It seemed so, as she returned to find him quizzing Miles about the capitals of Europe.

After dinner Miles disappeared to his room, while she served coffee in the lounge.

'You've only brought one cup,' Fen pointed out. 'Sit, and I'll fetch another.'

Clare stared at him bemusedly. She hadn't expected her presence at dinner to be extended to coffee afterwards.

'I——' She searched for an excuse, but he was already on his way out of the room.

He returned with the extra cup. Finding her still standing, he waved her into a comfortable armchair, then poured the coffee.

'Milk or cream?' he asked.

'Milk.'

'Sugar?'

'No...thank you,' she murmured politely as he handed her her coffee, then she sat uneasily at the edge of her chair. She wondered how quickly she might escape. This was all too egalitarian for her liking.

'About the driving lessons,' he said, taking the seat opposite.

'I really can't afford them,' she stated flatly.

'Fair enough.' He conceded the point. 'And you won't accept my funding them?'

'No,' she said rather shortly, adding a late, 'Thank you.'

'Then the solution's obvious,' he concluded on a dry note.

Clare frowned. It might be obvious to him, but not to her.

'I need a housekeeper who can drive,' he went on coolly and Clare's heart sank.

It was obvious now! She'd given him a good excuse. Bye, bye, Miss Anderson. It had been a very long day— a permanent job offer in the morning, the sack in the evening.

His voice cut into her thoughts. 'Pardon?' she blurted.

'I said,' he repeated with an exasperated edge, 'I'll give you lessons.'

'Lessons?' she echoed. 'Lessons in what?'

'Driving, of course.' His eyes accused her of being deliberately obtuse.

Clare continued to stare at him stupidly. *He* teach *her* to drive? Could he be serious?

'I taught my nephew Gerry—Lou's boy,' he relayed, as if giving his credentials, 'and you can't be any worse than he was. Like all seventeen-year-olds, he thought he was Nigel Mansell.'

'I—um——' Clare didn't know how to respond to this offer. It seemed hugely generous so she looked for the catch. 'I'm not sure it's such a good idea,' she finally said.

'Because we'd end up at each other's throats, you mean?' he suggested bluntly.

'No...well, perhaps...something like that,' she admitted slowly.

'It's possible,' he granted, 'but let's give it a try, at any rate.'

'I...all right,' Clare agreed, because she could do little else without making a fuss, but almost immediately regretted it.

She drank her coffee in seconds flat, then excused herself, so that she could retreat to the kitchen.

She spent the next few days with driving lessons on her mind. She dreaded them, although she couldn't quite say what she dreaded. His temper? In truth, she'd only seen him lose it that once at the railway station. His arrogance? To be fair, when she'd overheard him tutoring Miles, he was surprisingly patient and tolerant. So what was it that she dreaded?

She didn't work it out until the very first lesson. He didn't give her much warning. Having dropped Miles off at the riding school for the day, he returned to announce it was time for lesson number one.

'Are you sure? I haven't even started lunch.' She gave the best excuse she could find.

He shook his head. 'Forget lunch...I'll meet you outside in ten minutes.'

Given no choice, Clare reported to him as ordered. He was already there, sitting in the VW Golf he'd mentioned. To her relief, he installed her in the passenger seat.

'There's a disused airfield west of Oxford,' he relayed. 'I suggest we start by practising there.'

'All right.' Clare wasn't about to argue.

She sat in silence while he drove towards Oxford, and tried not to betray her nervousness. She wished now she'd agreed to pay for her own lessons.

'Here we are,' he announced as they finally went through some rusting gates that announced Byfield Sutton flying school.

In the distance there were airport hangars of corrugated iron, all very dilapidated. They had obviously been disused for some time.

'Are you sure we're not trespassing?' Clare asked worriedly.

He shrugged. 'We probably are, but I can't think anyone is around to prosecute ... So, try again,' he suggested with a slight smile.

'Sorry?' Clare blinked at him.

'To think of another excuse,' he added drily.

Clare pulled a face. She didn't like to be second-guessed, especially with such accuracy.

He continued to smile to himself as he drove towards the nearest runway. There were outgrowings of grass and weeds but the surface was fairly smooth. 'Right, let's swap seats. I'll get out.'

Reluctantly, Clare climbed over the gear-stick and sat behind the wheel, while he walked round. She told herself not to be nervous. She wasn't totally inexperienced. But it was Fen Marchand's instruction, not the driving that bothered her.

She waited for him to treat her like a brainless female, but he didn't. He went through the operation of the clutch, accelerator and brake a few times, giving clear, precise advice and instruction. He was not in the least bit patronising, and it made Clare realise once more that she didn't really know Fen Marchand.

'Got it?' he finally asked.

She nodded. 'I think so.'

'Right, ready for take-off?' He gave a small, wry smile of encouragement.

'Yes.' Clare stared at her feet, mentally sorting out brake, clutch and accelerator. For a moment she had a crisis of confidence and froze. If he'd said anything at that point, expressed any impatience, she'd have probably lost her nerve. But he made no comment, allowing Clare time to sort out the controls in her head.

She'd driven before, but not enough times for it to come naturally. Still, she started smoothly enough and drove in a reasonably straight line, actually changing up a gear, before he quietly asked her to stop.

'That was excellent for a first time.' His praise appeared quite genuine.

Clare felt a fraud. 'Not really. I have driven before.'

He frowned. 'I thought you said——'

'That I haven't a licence,' she rejoined, 'and I haven't, but I have driven a couple of times.'

'I see.' All the warmth went from his voice as he visibly stiffened.

'No, you don't!' Clare responded impetuously. 'You think I learned through joyriding, don't you? Or is it driving getaway cars?' Her exasperated tone ridiculed the idea. 'Well, neither's true, though I don't expect you to believe it.'

His eyes said as much as they caught and held hers, and tried to read the thoughts inside her head. 'So how *did* you learn?'

He still sounded suspicious. Clare felt like telling him to go take a jump, but then wondered if she was being fair. So he didn't trust her. Was that altogether surprising? All he knew about her was her criminal record.

'I had a friend,' she recounted briefly, 'who lived on an esta—farm... with its own roads. He let me drive his car a couple of times.'

It was the truth, but her hesitancy made it sound like a lie. She didn't like to talk of Johnny or that period in her life.

'What kind of car?' Fen Marchand asked.

Clare frowned at the question. What kind of car? Its male irrelevancy irritated her.

'I don't know.' She wasn't about to admit to having driven a Morgan V8, the very expensive toy of a very spoilt young man.

At the time it had seemed so exciting and romantic, touring round the estate with the soft top down and the evening breeze streaming back her long red hair. But it had always been at dusk or later, always well away from the main house, never when or where they might be spotted by The Family. She really had been a cheap thrill for Johnny.

Her bitter thoughts were reflected on her face, and Fen Marchand asked, 'What's wrong?'

She shook her head and quickly hid her feelings.

'Bad memories?' His eyes rested on her profile.

Clare heard what sounded close to compassion in his voice. She didn't want it. Her glance was dismissive.

'Mind your own business, Professor.' He said the words for her and smiled as her eyes winged back to him. 'You have a very expressive face—when you're not exercising rigid control, that is.'

'Snap!' Clare retorted before she could stop herself.

It was his turn to be surprised, but then he laughed aloud at her insolence.

'Two of a kind?' he suggested, before conceding, 'I suppose we are.'

He smiled at the idea, his guard down temporarily, and Clare couldn't help smiling back.

Her smile faded as their eyes caught and held, and her heart forgot to beat for a second or two. It was then that she realised what she'd dreaded. Not the lessons. Not driving. Not the professor's contempt. Or his anger. But this—a sudden, undeniable awareness of him as a man.

A beautiful man. A man most women would find attractive.

It was humiliating to find she was no exception.

'May we go home now?' she asked in a clipped voice, angry with herself, with him.

He frowned, as if he'd missed something in the conversation. He had, but then he wasn't included in the one going on in Clare's head.

'Back to the house, you mean?' he asked, and Clare mentally kicked herself for her slip of the tongue.

Woodside Hall wasn't home to her. It was just a place—a place she cleaned.

'You feel ready to drive on a main road?' He raised a challenging brow.

That wasn't what she'd meant and he knew it.

'Perhaps we'd better do a few turns of the airfield first?' he suggested with heavy irony.

Clare was left without any choice. She started the car, but this time crunched the gears with rough handling.

'Sorry,' she said automatically, unsure whether she was apologising to the car or him.

'Don't worry, relax,' he said in a kinder tone than she deserved. 'Just practise a few stops and starts, then drive around a little.'

With this, he sat back and gave every appearance of being at ease. He let her do things at her own pace and offered minimal instruction. On the few occasions she got into difficulties, his calm, unhurried manner got her out.

She had to admit it. He was a wonderful teacher. She had expected him to be supercilious and arrogant, and instead he was confidence-inspiring.

When she was competent in the mechanics of driving, he had her practise her mirror routine as if they were on a road with other vehicles.

'OK. Will we call it a day?' he suggested, just as her concentration was flagging. 'You've done very well.'

'Thanks.' Clare was pleased, despite herself, by his praise.

To her relief, they changed seats once more. Clare didn't feel ready for the open road yet.

She assumed he was driving home, until she caught a sign that told her they were travelling further into Oxford. 'Are we collecting Miles?' she asked.

'Later,' he nodded. 'First I thought we'd have lunch at a pub... There's not time to go back to Woodside.'

'Oh.' Clare's heart sank a little, but she didn't feel able to object.

He turned off the main road, and drove a couple of miles down narrower country lanes until they reached a public house called the Bargee's Rest. It stood on the Oxford canal and presumably had once been used by bargeman, but was now quite an up-market establishment.

They went through the pub to the restaurant at the rear. It was actually a long glass conservatory perched on a small hill, overlooking the canal and nearby lock gates. It was a beautiful location for lunch on a sunny August day.

Clare was woman enough to wish she were better dressed, but, as a waiter escorted them to a table, she didn't seem to be out of place among the diners who were holidaying on the canal cruisers lined up on the tow-path below.

Their fellow diners were obviously in holiday mood for there was quite a bit of laughter from other tables, but, despite the relaxed atmosphere, Clare was uncomfortably self-conscious.

She tried to remember the last time she'd lunched with a man, and realised she never had. Johnny had taken her nowhere during daylight hours, and, after Johnny, there had been just work and Peter.

Now, here she was, at twenty-six, on her first lunch date, with the handsomest man in the restaurant. Only it could hardly be called a date, when she was there purely because he couldn't leave her outside.

CHAPTER FIVE

AT FIRST she took refuge behind a menu and ordered a salad when the waiter came back.

'The food's fairly plain,' Fen said, perhaps feeling he had to make conversation, 'but very enjoyable.'

The comment cast a new doubt in Clare's mind. 'You must find my cooking even plainer.' She knew she was no master chef.

He shook his head, reassuring her, 'Having been brought up on a diet of boarding-school fodder, anything else seems positively exotic... And, believe me, I've eaten better in the last month than I have for a very long time.'

'Thanks.' Clare smiled, unable to resist such an emphatic compliment, even if it was only about her cooking. 'Did you enjoy boarding-school?' she asked out of genuine interest.

She half anticipated a yes, but he gave a short laugh, saying, 'Good lord, no! Only a masochist would have enjoyed the schools I attended.'

'Why, what was wrong with them?' Clare's curiosity was roused.

He rolled his eyes, as if to say, Everything! 'Well, my prep school was run on the "spare the rod and spoil the child" principle. Following that, my father paid extortionate fees to an establishment where everyone dressed like characters out of a Dickens novel, and bullying and snobbery were absolutely compulsory.'

Something triggered in Clare's memory, a documentary she'd once seen. 'Top hats and stiff collars?'

'Something like that,' he shrugged, pulling a face, before nodding. 'Just don't hold it against me, OK?'

'I'll try not to.' Clare matched his deadpan irony, and drew a smile of humour from him.

Clare was left once more wondering what made Fenwick Marchand tick. Most men who had been to schools like that boasted the fact. Clare seemed to remember the public school system had produced more prime ministers than any in the country.

'Is that where Miles will be going?' Clare knew it was traditional for fathers and sons to go to the same schools.

'Over my dead body! Even Miles at his worst doesn't deserve such a fate,' he declared drily, before running on, 'And, strangely enough, Miles hasn't been at his worst for some time... Since you came, in fact,' he finished meaningfully.

Clare's eyes went to his, unsure if she was being accused or congratulated. Either way, she felt uneasy.

'I've worked no miracles,' she said flatly.

'Haven't you?' The mood of the conversation suddenly turned serious. 'Since you came, he's been almost civilised, and certainly more enthusiastic about things.'

'Well, it has nothing to do with me.' Clare denied any influence on the boy.

His eyes narrowed on her expressionless face. 'I don't understand you. It's as if you don't want people to think well of you.'

He studied her across the table. Clare felt like an interesting specimen he couldn't quite classify.

'I just don't want people counting on me,' she replied, meaning to close the subject.

'Should I read that as some kind of warning?' he countered.

This time Clare shrugged in response. He could read it how he liked.

He looked ready to argue, then thought better of it, and took the hint, moving the conversation on to other, less controversial matters.

It was surprising how easily they could talk together, when they steered away from personal areas. They discussed the possible pleasures of a canal-boat holiday, one being the absence of television, and ended up debating the part the box had to play in the violence of their current society, with Clare arguing for censorship and Fen against. From there they moved on to civil liberties and politics, and, although the latter was his area, he was neither boring nor arrogant on the subject, but convincingly articulate.

'Have you ever thought of going in for politics?' Clare asked, impressed by his debating skills.

'I thought I had,' he responded drily, before running on, 'You mean party politics, getting elected for parliament and all that?'

Clare nodded. 'Yes, why not? I'm sure you have the necessary...' Clare searched for the correct word.

'Ego?' he suggested, laughing at himself.

Clare shook her head, and came up with, 'Presence.'

'Well, thank you, I think,' he said at the first compliment she'd ever offered him, 'but I'm afraid I lack other credentials...like drive, ambition, or sufficient self- or public interest. Not to mention anything remotely akin to political convictions,' he confessed with a dry laugh.

Clare frowned. 'I don't understand. You must have some convictions, surely. Politics is your subject.'

'Which is exactly why I should remain neutral,' he argued, 'rather than inflict my opinions on young, impressionable minds.'

'But you must *have* opinions,' Clare reasoned.

'Possibly,' he conceded with a smile, 'but none I feel a burning desire to share with my fellow man.'

Clare wasn't sure whether he was kidding or not. It was hard to tell. For a man in a serious, respected position, a professor at one of the foremost universities in the country, he seemed to take himself very unseriously. It was a likeable quality, Clare had to admit.

By dessert Clare was having great difficulty not relaxing in Fen Marchand's company. She had always seen him as the strong, silent type, but, in this mood, he was a witty, articulate companion, with a surprising, light-hearted, almost flippant side.

From politics they moved on to people-watching, as a sleek cabin cruiser joined a lengthy canal boat in the lock, and they tried to guess the professions of their respective owners.

'Teacher,' Clare suggested for the bespectacled forty-something organising his four children on the canal boat.

'Too many children,' Fen argued. 'Teachers don't have that number if they can possibly avoid it. I'd lay my money on a G.P. For some reason doctors have a compulsion to procreate.'

Clare smiled at his cynicism. When not directed at her, it was fairly amusing.

'And the one on the other boat?' She challenged his powers of deduction.

'Mmm.' He contemplated the younger man on the cruiser. He was dressed in cool Ray-Bans and spotless deck clothes, but looked wildly out of place, as though he should be in a city suit. 'Stockbroker, definitely.'

'How do you know?'

'Mobile phone sticking out of the back pocket,' Fen answered, laughing.

'You're kidding!' Clare assumed he was, pointing out, 'How can you see that? You're not wearing your glasses.'

'So? I'm short-sighted.' He stared at her intently for a moment, as if to prove it. 'I'm also wearing contacts.'

'Oh.' Clare stared back, as if to verify the fact, then wished she hadn't. She usually thought his blue eyes chilly. Today they brought a warm flush to her face.

He smiled a little, as if he could read her thoughts and feelings, before glancing downwards again. 'Anyway, look!' He nodded to the captain of the cabin cruiser. Unbelievably he was winding open the lock with one hand, while his other held a little portable phone to his ear. 'Probably checking on the latest price of gilts or futures or whatever. It's a form of addiction. My nephew Gerry is the same.'

'Louise's son.' Clare had heard of him in passing.

He nodded. 'Have you met him?'

'No, Mrs Carlton said he was in New York,' Clare recalled.

'For a year,' Fen confirmed, then gave her another speculative look, before saying, 'Which is probably just as well. From memory, you're just his type.'

'His type?' Clare echoed stiffly.

He wasn't discouraged, listing instead, 'Slim, long-legged, red-haired,' in a slightly dismissive tone.

'And what's yours?' Clare was prompted to ask, but immediately regretted it. This was no way to keep things on a master-servant footing.

'My type?' He paused as if giving it serious consideration. 'As a young man, I favoured soft, feminine, English-rose girls. But then I married one and had my illusions shattered,' he relayed with an edge of self-contempt. 'Nowadays, I suppose I prefer hard-headed career women who don't pretend to be otherwise... I'm not sure where you fit in,' he added with undercurrents that were difficult to interpret.

Nowhere, Clare would have thought. She was just his housekeeper, after all. So what was she doing, lunching with him? a voice inside her head asked.

'Well, I'd hardly call housekeeping a career,' she responded heavily, reminding them both of her position in life.

'No,' he agreed bluntly. 'So, what would you do for preference?'

Clare shrugged, then, because his interest seemed genuine, answered honestly, 'I think I've blown all my chances to do something else.'

'Why? Because of your prison record?' he said in normal conversational tones.

'Shh!' Clare forgot their respective positions and glared him into silence.

'Nobody heard,' he assured her, glancing round at their fellow diners. 'And, even if they did, I thought you didn't believe in apologising for your past.'

'I don't!' she declared, wondering if he was being purposely dense, 'but that doesn't mean I want it broadcast, either.'

'Fair enough.' He conceded the point, before asking again, 'So what would you do, given the chance?'

'I don't know.' Clare shrugged, but then saw no harm in admitting, 'Study, I suppose.'

'Study?' He raised a surprised brow. 'Study what?'

'Eighteenth-century English literature.' Clare specified what she spent much of her spare time reading.

It must have seemed a pretentious ambition for his first reaction was to laugh. When he saw her pained look, however, he quickly stopped. 'I'm sorry. It's just not what I expected.'

Clare bet it wasn't. He probably thought she could barely read, probably thought making a casserole taxed the height of her intellectual powers.

'I shouldn't have laughed,' he went on at her continued silence.

'Why not? It was just a joke, Professor.' Clare erected a tough, uncaring front once more.

'Was it?' He looked intently into her eyes, trying to read what was going on behind them.

'What else?' Clare gave a dismissive laugh to prove it, then stood up. 'Excuse me. I have to go to the toilet.'

'Clare.' He caught her arm as she went to pass him, and she was forced to stop. Strong male fingers curled round her wrist, holding her there. She looked down at him, her temper barely contained. He looked back at her, searching her face, before he admitted very quietly, 'I'm an insensitive idiot sometimes.'

'I—I——' Clare didn't know how to reply. His honesty took her breath away. She frowned more deeply, wishing he'd remain arrogant and difficult. She didn't want to like him.

He released his hold and in the end she said nothing, walking away instead. She retreated into her own ungraciousness.

'You're the idiot,' she told her own reflection in the toilet mirror, when she saw the high colour of emotion on her cheeks.

It was her own fault. He'd been making conversation. That was all. Why shouldn't he laugh, if she was silly enough to reveal unrealistic dreams? She was never going to get the chance to study, far less study something wildly impractical.

She was a housekeeper and lucky to be even that. She had to accept what she was, as her mother had before her. And, if she had any sense, she'd remember the fact, even when her employer decided to take an hour or two off and treat her as an individual.

When she returned to the table, there was no trace of the girl who had laughed so much over the meal. She refused his offer of coffee, and, realising things had changed, he followed her lead. He signalled for the bill and paid it with his credit card. She sat in silence and waited till he signed it.

Then she said with leaden politeness, 'Thank you for the meal, Professor.'

He shook his head, not wanting her gratitude. He looked as if he wished to say something else, his face a mixture of irritation and doubt, but she stood up, ready to go. He stood, too, and she walked ahead of him to the car.

They barely exchanged a word on the way to collect Miles. Clare felt a mixture of emotions. Part of her wished the lunch had never ended. For a little while she'd been like any young woman, enjoying the company of an intelligent, attractive man. For a little while she had forgotten her past and their respective positions and her determination to remain uninvolved. But it had been just that—a little while, a brief interlude from reality.

She had to keep her distance. She told herself that a dozen times in the days that followed. But it was impossible. The trouble was Fen Marchand himself. When she intentionally forgot to set an extra place at dinner, he didn't make an issue of it. He simply went to the antique dresser in the dining-room where the silver was kept, and set a place for her. And during the meal, although she tried to remain aloof, he insisted on including her in any conversation with Miles.

The driving lessons continued as well. After she obtained her provisional licence, he let her drive out on the public road. They went out almost on a daily basis, usually with Miles in the back. It was hard to refuse these lessons. He was doing her a favour and she did want to learn. He was a good teacher, too. So why object? Why listen to the voice inside her head, whispering warnings she didn't want to hear?

Was it so terrible that she was beginning to enjoy working for the Marchands—enjoy being a little happy after all the years of unhappiness? If she was beginning to like father as well as son, it didn't have to be a big deal. She wasn't a schoolgirl any more. She wasn't a fool. She wasn't going to lose her head over a man who could barely recall her surname and sometimes looked through her as if he'd forgotten her identity altogether.

She had a similar problem with him, at times. There were so many sides to Fen Marchand. When he was careless and flippant, she couldn't imagine him a serious professor of politics. But there were his books in the study to prove it. They weren't on obvious display, but interspersed with all the others and catalogued under subject. She'd taken one down once when he was out. Titled *From Chairman Mao to Tianenmen Square*, it was a political history of the Communist movement in China. The briefest perusal told her that Professor Marchand was a very learned man, yet he felt no need to impress the fact on people, and Clare had revised her original view of him as arrogant.

Nor was he a snob. It was just that umpteen genera-
tions of money had excluded his family from normal
everyday things. When Clare explained that she needed
to visit a supermarket to replenish their larder, he looked
a little at a loss.

'I've been shopping in the village,' she explained, 'and
that's all right for meat and vegetables, but it's over-
priced and limited for other goods.'

'Oh.' He'd obviously not given any thought to where
their supplies came from. He'd simply handed her over
a cash sum each week. 'Well, of course, I suppose I could
take you tomorrow... There must be a supermarket or
two in Oxford,' he reasoned after some consideration.

Clare wondered if he was kidding. He'd lived outside
Oxford almost all his life. Surely he'd visited a supermarket at some time?

It seemed not as he ran on, 'I'll phone Lou. She's
bound to know where one is... Will after lunch do?'

'Yes, fine.' Clare hid a smile at the thought of him
pushing a supermarket trolley.

Not that she really imagined he would. When he drove
her the next day, locating a supermarket with the help
of directions from his sister, Clare expected that he would
dump her at the door and collect her later. But no. He
locked up the Jaguar and followed her and Miles into
the store, and she almost gaped when he took the trolley
from her like a dutiful husband and trailed behind her
a couple of steps.

Perhaps because it was a novel experience for him,
not once did he adopt that martyred-husband I'd-rather-
be-somewhere-else look.

Clare had prepared a list and could have completed
the shopping quite quickly if she'd been on her own, but
Miles spent an age choosing his limited sweets al-
lowance, then spent another decade perusing a rack of
computer magazines. His father wasn't much better.
Having discovered a whole aisle of wines and spirits, he
stood studying labels for half an hour before selecting

a variety for his cellar. Eventually Clare left both males to their own devices while she shopped for essentials.

They met up at the check-outs. With his wine—the best and most expensive supplied by the supermarket—the bill was astronomical, but he didn't blink.

Afterwards they went for a coffee in the restaurant. Fen queued while they found a seat. Miles, having brow-beaten his father into purchasing a couple of magazines, promptly buried his nose in one. He barely looked up when his father placed his Coke in front of him and Fen raised his eyes to Clare.

'My son, the computer addict,' he commented with dry disapproval.

'There are worse ways he could spend his time,' Clare said in Miles's defence.

'Really?' Fen's tone was sceptical. 'You don't think we're raising a generation of computer-literate morons?'

He obviously did and Miles raised his head from his magazine to mutter, 'See! I told you.'

'Told you what?' Fen directed at Clare.

She frowned at Miles for landing her in this situation, but he took the easy way out, suddenly declaring a desperate need for the toilet. That left Clare with Fen's eyes trained on her, waiting for an answer.

'It was nothing, really,' Clare relayed, 'just that Miles once said you wouldn't buy him a computer because you thought they were "the death-knell of civilisation".'

He smiled at the quotation, not denying it. 'I take it you don't agree.'

'I don't know.' Clare shook her head. She was no expert on computers or civilisation. 'It just seems a bit...'

'A bit...?' He encouraged her to go on.

'Extreme,' Clare suggested carefully, wondering if she shouldn't just keep her opinions to herself.

'Probably,' he agreed, to her surprise, then grimaced. 'But Miles's relationship with his computer was extreme, too.'

'In what way?' Clare felt he'd invited her curiosity.

He hesitated a fraction, before admitting, 'Miles lived in L.A. for about nine months. His mother installed him, his computer and a Spanish maid in an apartment, then basically disappeared out of his life. The computer became his main companion.'

'God, he must have been lonely.' Clare's heart went out to the boy.

'That, and other things.' His eyes darkened at the memory. 'For the first few days he would barely talk to me. I had to prise him away from the computer and he quite literally suffered withdrawal symptoms... It's taken months for him to recover. In fact, he's only truly improved since you came.' He looked at her with undisguised gratitude.

Clare knew she should feel good about it, and she did a little. But a perverse side of her minded the fact that his acceptance of her stemmed from Miles's reactions. Underneath he probably still distrusted her.

'At any rate,' he continued, 'I am not really against computers *per se*. They have their uses and they're here to stay. Also, Miles has a natural aptitude for them. I just don't want to feed an obsession.'

Clare frowned, seeing his point of view. She suggested tentatively, 'You could always limit his time on it. Put it in a downstairs room, rather than his bedroom, and have set periods he's allowed on it.'

'I suppose.' He appeared to give the matter some consideration, but when Miles reappeared he said nothing.

It was later in the day, when dinner was over, that he raised the subject. Miles had already excused himself and was on his way out of the dining-room, when his father called him back.

'It's your birthday next week,' Fen said unsmilingly. 'Should I assume a computer is still your heart's desire?'

Miles nodded, but showed no excitement. He didn't expect he'd been getting his heart's desire.

'Well, your friend Clare——' he acknowledged her with a wry smile as she cleared the table '—has talked me round. Provided, of course, it doesn't interfere with your studies, that you aren't on it longer than an hour a day, and that you don't just use it for mindlessly violent computer games.'

'I won't. I promise.' A grin appeared from ear to ear on the boy's face as he realised what his father was saying. 'Thanks, Dad,' he said quickly, remembering his manners, but it was Clare he went up to and gave a quick, impulsive kiss on the cheek, before saying, 'Thanks, Clare. You're great.'

For a moment she was taken aback, then she smiled at the boy, touched by the gesture.

As Miles bounced from the room, his father murmured something that sounded like, 'Lucky him.'

Clare couldn't believe she'd heard properly, but her cheeks went pink, and she got on with gathering the dirty crockery to hide her confusion.

She went through to the kitchen, and he followed, carrying dishes, too. She ignored him, but she sensed him watching her as she made the coffee. She set a tray for one.

'Join me,' he said in a quiet voice.

Clare wasn't sure if it was an order or a request. She treated it as the latter, saying, 'No, thanks. It's been a long day and I'm tired.'

'All right.' He didn't seem too concerned until she picked up his coffee-tray, about to carry it through to the lounge. He took it from her hands, muttering in annoyance, 'I can wait on myself.'

Clare pulled a face at his back. There was no pleasing some people.

She couldn't believe he was really bothered whether she kept him company or not, yet later, in her attic rooms, she reflected how similar their lives were in their solitude. Since her arrival, he'd had no visitors, no dinner guests, no girlfriends. She assumed it was through choice, and wondered if one disastrous marriage had made him wary.

She discovered differently, however, the next evening, when he asked her to keep Miles company for dinner so that he could go out.

'Where's he gone?' Miles asked when they sat in the kitchen together, having their meal.

'I don't know,' Clare shrugged.

'Didn't you ask?' the boy added, slightly disgruntled.

'Hardly,' she replied shortly. Like his father, Miles seemed to forget at times that she was a servant in the house, not a member of the family.

'Oh, no!' the boy suddenly exclaimed. 'I bet it's her.'

'Her?' she echoed automatically.

'Professor Millar.' He pulled a face. 'His girlfriend. She's a lecturer in history. Mega-boring!'

'Miles!' Clare reproved, wondering if he meant history or the girlfriend.

'Well, she is,' he insisted. 'Wait till you meet her.'

Clare wasn't sure if she wanted to meet Fen Marchand's girlfriend. She definitely didn't want to analyse the sinking feeling in her stomach.

She told herself to stop being so stupid. She should have known anyone as physically attractive as Fen Marchand would have a girlfriend. Why should it matter to her?

'I'm sure she's perfectly pleasant,' she said, regaining some of her composure.

'Have you ever seen *101 Dalmations*?' Miles asked, and, at her nod, added, 'Well, she makes Cruella de Ville seem like Mary Poppins.'

'Miles!' Clare gave him another reproving look. She assumed he was exaggerating, jealous of his father's attention going elsewhere.

Weren't they both? The thought crept into Clare's head, but she pushed it right back out again. Fen Marchand could date whom he liked. It wasn't her concern.

Miles said as much, muttering, 'It's all right for you. She's not going to be your stepmother... I wish she'd stayed in America.'

America? That explained things, Clare thought. Explained why she'd never been mentioned. Presumably she'd been away for a while. Well, it was none of her business.

But it didn't stop Clare thinking, wondering, waiting for the professor to return home. Only he didn't, and she fell asleep watching the clock.

She was woken between midnight and one by the sound of a car. She assumed it was Fen returned, but then realised the car was driving away from the house. She climbed out of bed and went to the window, in time to see tail-lights disappearing down the drive.

It couldn't be Fen. He'd left in his own car, and there was no sign of it in the yard. So who else could it be?

Burglars. The idea crept into her head, and refused to creep out again.

Of course, it would be just her luck. The one night he goes out and the house gets burgled. It wasn't hard to work out who'd be the prime suspect.

Clare told herself to go back to bed and stay there. If the family silver, or the first editions, or his landscapes had gone walkabout, did she want to be the one to discover the fact? She imagined telephoning the police, only to be interviewed, doubted, arrested. No, thank you.

Go back to bed, she told herself. It was the wise thing to do. But then wisdom didn't figure largely in Clare's make-up, and duty compelled her to do otherwise.

She put a raincoat over her pyjamas as a dressing-gown, and climbed down the attic steps. She checked on Miles first, and found him sound asleep. Warily she took the main staircase and went to the front door. The lights were on but she'd left them on. There was no sign of forced entry. On the contrary, where she'd left the door locked, it was now bolted. Someone was in the house.

She froze as a voice behind her asked, 'Going somewhere?'

She didn't have to turn to recognise its owner. She turned all the same, because she had no other choice. She could hardly stand there for the rest of the night, wishing she'd ignored her conscience.

She found Fenwick Marchand in the open doorway of the lounge, a glass in his hand.

His eyes swept down her, taking in the pink cotton pyjamas underneath her coat.

'Shouldn't you have dressed first?' he enquired in the same sarcastic tone. 'Or is that perhaps appropriate dress for a rendezvous?'

'Rendezvous?' Clare repeated stupidly.

'Assignation. Tryst. Meeting,' he suggested like a walking dictionary, then laughed low in his throat.

Clare stared at him warily. She didn't know him in this mood.

'You think I'm meeting someone?' she finally said, her tone denying the fact.

'Well, you're hardly going jogging in that outfit,' he responded.

'I...it's not how it looks,' Clare claimed, not very originally.

'Really?' He raised a brow in disbelief. 'Surprise me, then.'

Clare realised it was an invitation to tell the truth, but her burglar fears now seemed absurd. In fact, she might put ideas in his head as to why *she'd* been creeping about his house at this hour.

Marchand's mouth formed a sneer at her silence, then with a mutter that sounded distinctly like, 'To hell with it,' he disappeared back into the lounge.

Clare was disconcerted. She didn't quite know what to do next. She followed him into the lounge. He was standing by the cocktail cabinet, pouring himself another drink.

He must have sensed her presence, as he said, without turning, 'Want one?'

He gestured towards a nearly empty bottle of whisky. It had been half-full when Clare had cleaned the cabinet that morning.

'No, thank you.' Clare's tone echoed her distaste.

'Ah, yes, I forgot,' he drawled, 'you don't drink. You don't smoke. What *do* you do?'

'Nothing,' she claimed shortly.

'*Nothing*?' His eyes travelled from her face to her pyjama nightwear beneath the coat. 'Well, it's hardly the most seductive of outfits, but I don't suppose he'll care.'

'And just who do you imagine this "he" to be?' Clare responded, more in exasperation than anything else. 'The milkman? The postman? Or perhaps the paper boy. Because they're the only men I've met in the last month,' she pointed out.

'So?' He dismissed her argument in one word. 'I imagine you had a lover or two in your, shall we say, *colourful* past?'

Clare's face suffused with anger. He really did see her as some good-time girl. Perhaps all men would, simply because she'd once been in prison. The way Marchand looked at her was the way she imagined men looked at prostitutes.

Her green eyes blazed her dislike of him. She held his stare as he closed the gap between them.

'So, tell me—how many?' He did not hide his own contempt. 'Five? Ten? Twenty? Or can't you remember?'

'Why, you——' Clare's hand lifted automatically, and was caught before it made contact.

'Uh-uh, once was enough,' he said, and held her with ease as she tried and failed to twist her wrist from his grip.

Then he dragged her so close that she smelled the faintest odour of whisky beneath the male scent of his aftershave. Neither smell was unpleasant but she still flinched away from him.

He growled at her, 'Do I repel you that much?'

Clare didn't answer. His mood seemed suddenly dangerous. She pulled and pulled at his grip, not caring that she hurt herself in the process.

He caught her other arm, and, holding her still, ground out, 'Stop panicking! I'm not going to rape you.'

He sounded more his usual superior self.

'I may not have had a woman for a while,' he added bluntly, 'but I'm not that desperate.'

And, presumably he'd have to be, Clare thought, to want her. She felt the insult like a slap, and wanted to hurt back.

She found herself sneering in return, 'Neither's your ladyfriend, it seems.'

It wiped the supercilious expression right off his face.

'Ladyfriend?' His eyes narrowed, but if they held a warning Clare ignored it.

'The one you were out with,' she went on recklessly. 'Didn't she want to come in for *coffee*?'

Clare guessed that was who'd driven home. It was obvious why. He was already over the limit.

'Let's get this right,' he ground back. 'You think I've been out with someone and been…dumped. Would that be the correct word in your social set?'

His sarcasm was meant to be withering, but Clare wasn't so easily withered. 'Look, don't take your frustration out on me!' she retorted recklessly.

She'd gone too far. She realised that from his face, even before his arm shot out and caught her again.

'You think I can't make a woman want me?' Low and intense, the question made Clare lose her nerve. She tried to break free, but couldn't. 'Let's see, shall we?'

She realised what he intended, and turned away just in time. She started to struggle, but he held her easily. A hand went to the back of her hair, forcing her head up.

If she'd been more experienced, Clare might have known how to handle the situation, but there had been no one before Johnny, and no one after, and their lovemaking had always been a light, sweet thing.

But this wasn't lovemaking. It wasn't even sex. Just pain and humiliation.

As his mouth ground down on hers, a cry rose in her throat. His teeth forced her lips to part and his tongue thrust into her mouth. She sobbed aloud and tried once more to turn her face. He held her there, kissing her, hurting her, frightening her, until tears started to roll down her face.

Then all of a sudden he stopped. His mouth left hers. His arms relaxed their punishing hold. She stared up at him, with a mixture of accusation and fear, and he stared back at her, his face shadowed, drained of anger. It was clear that he had gained no pleasure from the kiss.

'It seems you were right.' His mouth twisted with the bitterness of self-loathing. 'I know more of hurting than loving. Perhaps I always did.'

'I...' Clare heard echoes of past pain and future despair, and fear left her.

She raised her eyes and saw the stark truth in his. She had thought him hard and unfeeling, and perhaps he was. But they had travelled down the same road. They had loved once, and would never love again.

'I'm sorry.' The words slipped from her lips before she could stop them.

'Don't pity me!' he rasped at her, and would have turned from her if she hadn't stopped him.

Clare had thought all compassion, all weakness inside her, had died with Peter. But her once gentle spirit was there in her eyes, there in her touch, as she reached out to him.

He looked down at the small white fingers gripping his arm. He might have pushed her away, but a look of hurt crossed her face. He saw it and took her hand instead.

The contact jolted her a little. She had acted impulsively, without thought of how he might respond. He held her hand in his, their eyes locked, and her heart stopped for a beat. He lifted her hand to his cheek. His skin was warm and dry, but rough, too, in need of a shave. Something stirred deep inside her.

He moved his head slightly until his mouth touched the palm of her hand. It was more intimate, more potent than any kiss of anger. Slowly his lips traced her lifeline, tasted her skin, and she felt the treacherous pull of desire.

She shut her eyes and tried to voice a protest. Before she could, he took his mouth away and laid her hand against his shoulder. She drew an unsteady breath, then felt reason slipping away as his lips pressed against her temple. He held her lightly, one hand clasping hers, the other at her waist. She could have broken away, could have fought against the slow, insidious pleasure flowing through her. But, though her mind cried out, Not with him, please, not with him, her senses reeled.

When his lips trailed down her cheek, she remained paralysed. When his mouth touched hers, she gave a small moan of protest. 'No, don't...' But it was very weak, a whisper against his lips, a breath touching his, less than nothing. Little wonder he ignored it, as her lips parted to his, and she, too, sought the oblivion of passion.

She forgot who he was. She forgot who *she* was. She forgot everything as she remembered the way love had once been. She remembered the sweet rush of a mouth covering hers, the warmth of another body so close, the urgency of male hands as they drew her softness even closer.

It had been so long since she'd been held, she had no resistance. He kissed her gently at first, and she trembled with desire. He kissed her harder, betraying need, and she responded with a passion that shook them both.

They kissed until her head swam and her senses reeled and she had to cling to his shoulders so that she wouldn't

fall. She barely noticed when he took her in his arms
and pressed her back against the settee. He kept kissing
her, making her feel, need, forget. She wasn't aware of
his hand pushing aside her coat until his fingers started
to unbutton her pyjama-top.

Then he lifted his mouth from hers and she opened
her eyes. They looked at each other and remembered
what they had forgotten. He was Fenwick Marchand,
her employer. She was Clare Anderson, his servant.

But it didn't seem to matter to him. He lowered his
head, and, before she could stop him, took the rosy bud
of her nipple in his mouth. It sent such a shudder of
desire through Clare, she almost forgot again. Slowly
he circled the nipple with his tongue, then gently sucked
on her hard, aching flesh. She felt a sweet agony spread
through her body, spasm through her loins, and wanted
to press her soft flesh to the hardness of his. But she
forced herself to hold on to reality, to see herself as he
must—a girl with no morals, of no importance—and
pride overcame her weakness.

'No!' The word was torn from her, clear and cutting
and final, as she pushed at his shoulders and started to
panic.

She didn't need to. He heard and understood. He
cursed with frustration as he lifted his head away, but
he accepted her right to change her mind. He rolled off
her and stood up, away from her.

His breathing was ragged. So was hers. He watched
as she drew her clothes round her, and rose to her feet.

'I'm sorry.' She apologised once more, feeling she had
led them to this point.

He shook his head. 'Don't be. It was just sex,' he
dismissed.

'Just sex'. Clare silently echoed his words and felt a
wave of humiliation. He was right, of course. Just sex.
But surely that made it worse.

'It's one of life's little ironies,' he continued as he
picked up his glass and took a stiff drink from it. 'We

don't really know each other, and, at times, we don't even seem to like each other. But it doesn't stop me wanting you, wanting to take you upstairs to my bed, wanting to...' He trailed off and let his eyes say the rest. They caught and held hers, and once more Clare felt a deep elemental attraction to this man. He was right. She could go upstairs with him now, and let him pleasure her, and want to pleasure him, and feel more alive than she had for a long time. And perhaps, because there was no love, there would be no pain. And no joy and no meaning. Just sex, as he said.

'I...' She shook her head, her eyes dark hollows in her thin face, and started to back away.

He laughed at her, at himself. 'Go on, run. I won't follow. I'm probably too drunk, anyway.'

Clare hesitated, struggling with an inexplicable guilt. It was as if she was turning her back on a drowning man. Perhaps she was, as he raised his glass to his lips and drained it.

She stood there until he turned his back on her, and, clearly dismissing her from his thoughts, poured himself another drink.

Then she fled upstairs, wishing she had never come down, never realised her own weakness or seen his. She didn't want to feel anything. She didn't want to be free from the cold, empty prison where her heart now lay. She had sentenced herself to a life without love. She wanted no pardon.

CHAPTER SIX

'I'M SORRY about last night,' Fenwick Marchand said when he appeared mid-morning in the kitchen.

Clare turned from the sink in surprise. She'd been dreading breakfast but only Miles had arrived at the table, then gone out to his den in the woods.

She didn't answer Fen. She didn't really want to talk about last night. She'd hoped he'd pretend it hadn't happened.

'I had too much to drink at my college dinner,' he admitted bluntly.

Clare flinched inwardly. She understood what he was saying. Sober, he would never have made a pass at her.

'It won't happen again,' he went on to assure her.

'No,' Clare agreed shortly, and made herself look him straight in the eye. She wanted him to understand she was no push-over.

He got the message. 'You don't give much away, do you?'

What did he expect? Clare wondered. Her to be grateful for his apology?

'Forget it,' she clipped back. 'I have.'

His brows rose a little. 'I didn't realise I was so unmemorable.'

There was almost a suggestion of humour in his voice, but it fell on stony ground. Clare wanted a return to strict formality between them.

'Anyway,' he continued at her silence, 'I just want you to understand that last night was...shall we say...an aberration? I have no plans to play Mr Rochester to your Jane.'

It was Clare's turn to raise a brow. Did he think her so stupid that she mistook sex for romance?

He certainly thought her stupid as he felt the need to add, 'Jane Eyre. It's a book——'

'By Charlotte Brontë,' Clare cut in before he could make her out to be a complete fool. 'I *have* read it . . . I can read, you know,' she told him heavily.

'Of course. I didn't mean to be patronising.' He surprised her once more by apologising.

Clare wondered why he was being so reasonable. Her eyes narrowed on him in suspicion. He was wearing his reading glasses; behind them, his normally sharp blue eyes reflected the effects of a heavy night's drinking. But, even blurred at the edges, he was still too handsome. He returned her scrutiny and she looked away.

She took refuge in activity, reaching for the electric kettle and filling it. With her back to him, she asked, 'What would you like for breakfast?'

'Black coffee, strong,' he requested with a certain irony in his voice. 'I'll have it in my study.'

'Certainly,' she answered without turning, and was glad when she heard his retreating footsteps.

He paused in the doorway to say, 'When you see Miles, please send him to me,' then disappeared.

Clare let out the breath she'd been holding since she'd risen that morning. She had dreaded their first meeting; she had expected that, sober, he would treat her with derision. She hadn't anticipated an apology, especially one so freely given, but it was a relief. The incident was to be forgotten, the subject closed, and things would go back to a formal footing.

To a certain extent, things did. They managed to put on a good show for Miles on his birthday, when he finally got the longed-for computer. The driving lessons stopped, or at least his personal tution did. Instead he hired a professional driving instructor and overruled her objections by saying, 'I need a housekeeper who can drive.'

He gave her little choice so she accepted the lessons and, if her condescendingly smooth instructor made her appreciate her former teacher, she kept these thoughts to herself.

She'd assumed also that she would no longer be dining with the family, but he still insisted on it, and, with Miles as chaperon, the meals passed pleasantly enough.

But much of the time Clare was aware of undercurrents between them. It might be a word or a look or a gesture, and she found herself remembering how it had felt, in his arms, his mouth on hers, his hard body close. No amount of self-discipline could control these thoughts, her feelings, and the warning they held was stark: she should leave.

The trouble was she didn't want to. After the monotonous, meaningless regime of prison, and the underlying violence, life at Woodside Hall tasted sweet. If there was a certain ambivalence in her relationship with Fen, he also treated her with an odd respect. Would another employer, knowing her prison record? And there was Miles. From a truculent, unhappy youngster, he was slowly turning into a bright, open boy, and, though she was still determined to remain uninvolved, her feelings for him had definitely grown to fondness. If he hung round her much of the day, she didn't mind.

She wondered sometimes, however, if his father minded. He never said anything. He never tried to discourage Miles or send him elsewhere. It was just his expression when he caught them in the kitchen, chatting or laughing together. Clare read it as worry as to what things she might be teaching his son, but, as he never came out and said as much, she could hardly challenge him.

Clare still resented it. She was always scrupulously careful not to influence Miles. She might listen to his complaints—someone needed to—but she never voiced an opinion. The most she did was advise Miles on how best to approach his father.

On the subject of boarding-school he complained more and more, as the prospect drew nearer. 'I'm not going, and he can't make me,' he declared one day, clearly rehearsing his bolshiness with Clare.

'He can, Miles,' she warned him quietly, 'so I wouldn't take that attitude. Why don't you just try explaining *why* you don't want to go...? It's the boarding part that scares you, isn't it?'

The boy's eyes were guarded, but she'd obviously hit on the truth. 'I'm not scared of leaving home or anything. I just don't want to spend every second of the day with a bunch of stupid English schoolboys.'

Clare's brows lifted. She wondered how Miles visualised himself—obviously not in the same category.

'How do you get on with other boys?' she asked outright.

He scowled a little, then said grudgingly, 'All right. I can make friends, if I want to. I just don't bother much.'

It was a defensive response, and betrayed traces of insecurity. Clare looked hard at Miles and he looked away, but not before she'd caught sight of a very lonely little boy.

'You'd prefer to go to a normal day school,' she concluded for him.

'Yes,' he admitted.

'Then tell your father that,' she suggested.

'Oh, yeah?' He looked sceptical. 'You think it would make a difference?'

'I don't know,' she responded, 'but it's worth a try, isn't it? Just make sure you're polite about it.'

Miles considered her words for a moment, then shrugged. But, as he rose from the table, he muttered something that could just have been, 'Thanks,' before disappearing.

She'd all but forgotten their chat when she served breakfast the next morning.

'Father.' Miles's voice suddenly broke the silence and caused both adults to look at him in surprise.

It was the first time Clare had heard him use the word 'father'. It seemed a very English form of address from a boy who so often adopted an American accent.

It certainly attracted Fen Marchand's attention as he lowered his newspaper and waited.

'Father,' Miles repeated, now that he had his audience, 'I've been giving some thought about school. I'm not sure I'm ready for boarding-school, especially as my education has been rather...erratic in the last year or two,' he announced solemnly.

Erratic? Clare raised mental eyebrows at his choice of words.

His father continued to stare at his son over the top of his glasses.

Clare could see he was struggling to reconcile this polite, reasonable boy with the Miles who often confronted him. Miles had obviously taken her advice and rehearsed his speech, going a little overboard on the politeness angle. She hoped Fen would hear him out.

'Go on,' Fen invited with an unreadable calm.

'I thought...' Miles wavered a little at his father's deadpan expression, looked to Clare for encouragement, and, receiving an almost imperceptible nod, went on, 'I thought it might be better if I just went to a local school.'

'Really?' His father didn't betray his feelings as he asked, 'Have you somewhere in mind?'

Miles shook his head. 'I'd go anywhere you chose. You'd not have to worry about me. I could cycle there and back, easy. And I could let myself in the house if no one was home. And I swear you'll hardly notice I'm here,' he promised earnestly.

His eyes pleaded with his father to listen and revealed a desperation that pulled at Clare's heart. She'd realised he hated the idea of boarding-school; she hadn't realised till now just how much.

Would Fen understand? She glanced at him but his expression was still unreadable.

She half expected him to dismiss Miles's appeal out of hand. Instead he said, 'I'm sorry, Miles, but it's not that easy. Sometimes I have to work late, and you can't possibly remain alone in the house. Even if it were advisable—which it's not—it is actually illegal for a boy of your age to be on his own.'

'There's Clare,' Miles said in desperation; 'she would be in. She could look after me.'

'Yes, well...' Fenwick Marchand's eyes slid to Clare and obviously found her wanting. He didn't say so outright, however, instead choosing to argue, 'That's not feasible, either. Clare is here to housekeep, not babysit, and, with her working morning and evening, she can hardly be expected to look after you in the afternoons, too.'

'I won't need looking after,' Miles denied, and, eyes pleading with Clare now, added, 'All she'd need to do was let me in the house and I could hang out in my room.'

'That would still demand that she remain in the house every afternoon,' Fen pointed out.

'But that's all right. She never goes anywhere usually, anyway. Do you, Clare?' His face begged her to agree.

'Well, no,' she conceded, accepting that she spent most of her free time in her room, reading.

'So, you could always pay her a little more so she wouldn't mind staying in,' Miles reasoned, 'and I wouldn't bother her, so she'd still have her break. And I wouldn't bother you, either, when you got home... And you'd save a fortune on school fees,' he put in with the skill of a born negotiator.

Clare looked from him back to his father, holding her breath for his reaction. She doubted if any of Miles's arguments washed with Fenwick Marchand. Money was hardly a consideration for him and it had to be more

convenient to send Miles away, yet he seemed reluctant
just to dismiss the boy's request out of hand.

'Please,' Miles added in a voice that would have melted
the hardest of hearts.

It even seemed to have an effect on Fen although it
didn't exactly draw the desired response.

'You're going to have to give me time to consider this,
Miles,' he finally said.

Miles's face went tight and unhappy as he read his
father's answer as a no. He looked to Clare and almost
exploded the word, 'See!' at her as he pushed back his
chair. He'd left the kitchen before either adult could stop
him.

Perhaps Fen Marchand was used to Miles's sudden
departures because he barely reacted. Instead he turned
quizzical eyes on Clare.

'*See*?' he echoed his son. 'See what exactly?'

'I—um—— Look, this has nothing to do with me.'
She rose to collect the dirty plates.

'Sit!' he commanded abruptly and, in her surprise,
Clare automatically obeyed.

But then pride made her mutter, 'I'm not a dog, you
know.'

'No,' he agreed, 'and I'm not a monster, but my son
and you obviously think I am . . . So let's hear it. Whose
idea is day school?'

'Miles's, of course,' Clare claimed. 'I just advised him
to discuss it with you.'

His brows rose in disbelief.

'That's *all* I did,' she insisted. 'He told me he didn't
want to go to boarding-school and I suggested he talk
over his reasons with you.'

'Well, that has to be a first—Miles taking anyone's
advice,' he conceded in an almost wry tone. 'You seem
to have quite an influence over my son.'

Bad influence, Clare assumed he meant, and her
lips pursed. 'I simply *listen* to him,' she said with
inherent criticism.

He got the point quickly, muttering, 'And I don't?' but then surprised her by admitting, 'Perhaps you're right, but he doesn't make it easy... Is he really so against boarding-school?'

Clare nodded but said no more.

'Look,' he pursued, 'if you know how he feels, tell me.'

She hesitated a moment, then blurted out, 'All right, he's scared.'

'*Scared*? Scared of what?' His voice hardened in anger.

Clare realised her mistake and decided to give up, there and then. 'I don't know... I have to clear up.'

She rose once more and started to collect the dirty crockery. He rose, too, and, taking the plates from her hand, tossed them into the kitchen sink. A cup broke but he didn't seem to notice as he forced her to turn and face him.

'Uh-uh, you can't make a statement like that then retreat behind model-servant role when it suits.' He stood between the sink and the table, blocking off her exit route, and waited. 'If it's immunity you want, you have it.'

'Immunity?'

'From being sacked.'

Clare raised her eyes to his, not concealing her distrust. He looked cool and implacable, but she knew from experience that he had a temper.

'What's Miles scared of?' He reminded her of the question she'd evaded.

Clare felt he'd asked for it, and told him bluntly, 'Of being a misfit?'

'A *misfit*?' His face went even more rigid, but he insisted, 'Go on!'

Clare felt she might as well. She'd already gone much further than good sense dictated.

'Miles doesn't know who he is or who he wants to be. For the first seven or eight years of his life he lived here with you and was probably expected to behave like a little adult,' she guessed from her own observations. 'After that he went to live with a grandfather who gave him everything but his time. Then his mother had him and, from his own accounts, let him do what he liked, as long as he kept out of her way.

'Now he's back here with you,' Clare continued bravely, 'and he's expected to return to behaving like a model little Englishman... Well, he isn't. He's too messed up for that. And he hasn't a hope of fitting into some nice upper-class boarding-school. He knows it, even if you don't!' she concluded bluntly.

Until that moment, Clare hadn't realised just how angry she felt about Miles and the way he'd been treated. Conviction had rung in every unwise word she'd uttered.

She watched Fen's face, half expecting fury in reaction. She'd more or less told him he was a poor father.

For a moment he seemed unaffected, then he closed his eyes. It was the merest flicker of emotion on a face that rarely showed any, but Clare saw it and wished then that she had kept her opinions to herself.

'I'm sorry. I shouldn't have said——' She reached a hand out.

He stepped back, too proud to accept any consolation. 'Don't apologise. I asked for the truth, you gave it. If I don't like it, that's my problem.'

Clare was surprised once more by this man. She thought of him as unemotional and insular, and he was. But he had qualities of fairness and strength that she couldn't help admiring.

'Presumably you think a day school would be better.' His tone held no trace of sarcasm, as if he really did want her opinion.

So Clare gave it. 'Yes, much better. He's still going to have problems making friends, but this way he'll be able to come home and talk about it.'

He nodded. 'I'd originally planned for him to attend Sir Thomas Arnold's, an independent in Oxford,' he admitted, 'but when I couldn't keep a housekeeper boarding-school seemed the sensible option. Perhaps Arnold's could still find a place for him.' He was obviously thinking aloud, and Clare remained silent, sure that he didn't intend to include her in any decision-making. She was taken aback when he added, 'However, it all very much depends on you—whether you're prepared to supervise him out of school hours.'

'I—I... Well, if you want me to...' Clare was sure she must have misunderstood.

Fen misread her hesitation, saying, 'Never mind, I shouldn't have asked. You have enough to do with the housekeeping. I'll have to work out some alternative.'

He turned away as if to go, and she caught at his sleeve.

'No, listen, it's not that,' she declared rashly. 'I'm quite happy to look after him. I was just surprised, that's all... I mean, your wanting *me* to do it.'

'Why not you? You seem to understand Miles better than most people, including me,' he admitted, pulling a face.

'I just thought... well, with my record...' She wondered if he'd momentarily forgotten her background.

'That I wouldn't trust you?' he asked, and she nodded grimly. 'I've already trusted you round my home for two months. I assume that if you'd intended to abscond with the family silver you would have done so by now.'

'Thanks.' It was hardly an unequivocal vote of confidence, although Clare supposed she couldn't expect more.

'Anyway, my sister has sufficient faith in you to guarantee replacement of any items that do walk,' he admitted drily.

Clare's face flushed red. Just for a moment or two, as they talked of Miles, she'd almost felt he was treating her like an equal. Now she realised she was a calculated risk against which he was insured.

'Of course, my sister believes you were innocent,' he added, scepticism in his tone.

Clare ignored it. At least Louise believed in her.

'Were you?' Fenwick stared down at her, his eyes intent behind his glasses.

Something compelled her to tell the truth. 'Not really, no.'

He looked surprised by her answer, then gave a short laugh. 'Well, that's honest, at any rate. I suppose you told Lou what she wanted to hear.'

Clare shook her head. 'Louise and I have never discussed my conviction.'

'I see. How typical of Louise,' he drawled, with both fondness and exasperation. 'She imagines that because she likes someone they can't possibly do anything bad.'

'Is that so awful?' Clare felt a need to defend Louise Carlton.

'No, just not very realistic.' He looked hard at her, as if he might read the truth in her eyes, then added speculatively, 'Personally I think most of us are capable of doing just about anything, given a specific set of circumstances.'

He was right. Clare knew that from her own experience. But if it was an invitation to confess, she didn't take it up. Instead she lifted her head slightly and held his stare, refusing to betray her secrets.

'I won't steal from you.' She felt that was all he needed to know.

She didn't expect him to believe her, but he nodded slightly before saying, 'Fair enough ... So let's return to the original issue—Miles. Are you willing to monitor him between school and my return from work?'

Monitor him? Clare's brows rose mentally. Miles didn't want someone to monitor him. He needed someone to provide him with lemonade and cake, and listen to his day, good or bad. Clare wasn't sure if she should be the person, but right at the moment there was no one else.

'Yes,' she answered briefly.

'Good,' he said, nodding to himself. 'I'll pay you extra, of course. I'll have to find out the correct rate.'

Clare shrugged. She wasn't going to argue with him. By paying her, he kept it on a 'me master, you servant' level, and that suited them both. The fact that Miles already hung about her for quite a bit of the day seemed to have escaped his notice. At least now she was going to be paid for it.

'I'd prefer you didn't mention things to Miles until I've secured a place for him at Arnold's,' he added unnecessarily.

'Will it be difficult?' she asked. 'School starts in two weeks.'

'I'm not sure. I do know one of the governors,' he relayed. 'She's in the history department of my college. It was she who recommended the school. I'll ring her now,' he said distractedly, and headed for the door. He stopped there for a moment and turned to add, 'I should thank you for your advice.'

Clare shook her head. 'I'd wait and see if it's any good. With Miles, it's difficult to say what's the best thing,' she declared rather frankly.

He grimaced in agreement. 'Quite,' he said, before leaving the room.

They did not mention the subject for a few days, then one morning after breakfast he said, 'I have an interview this afternoon with Miles's prospective headmaster. I wondered if you could look after him for a couple of hours.'

'Yes, of course,' she agreed without hesitation. She had begun to question if he'd had second thoughts about leaving her in charge of Miles. It pleased her that he hadn't. She had been treated as a criminal for three years, and it felt good to be trusted again.

'There is a problem, however,' he added, and her spirits sank a little. 'I promised to go riding with him today.'

'Yes, he told me.' The boy had been looking forward to it all of yesterday.

'So he may be somewhat…resentful…at missing out,' Fen pointed out.

Clare thought that was the understatement of the year. 'Why don't I take him?' she suggested the obvious.

'You?' He frowned blankly. 'Take him riding, you mean?'

She nodded, wondering why he should look so surprised.

'Well, that's good of you, Clare…' he chose his words with care '…but I don't think that's feasible. It's not just a matter of delivering him at the stables. He would have to be supervised.'

'I can supervise him,' she shrugged.

'On horseback, I mean,' he said slowly, as if he was dealing with an inferior intellect.

Which he probably was. After all, she didn't have a Ph.D. in political history. But she wasn't totally without sense or talent.

'I *can* ride,' she reminded him drily, 'or I wouldn't have offered.'

'Yes, of course. I forgot.' He looked at her over the top of his glasses, as if he was wondering what other things he might discover about her. 'Where did you learn again?'

'Well, not at Her Majesty's pleasure,' she said, knowing he believed prison to be some sort of holiday camp. 'I used to muck out at racing stables when I was Miles's age, then, later on, I exercised the horses.'

His brows rose in surprise. 'You must be a fairly competent rider, then.'

She shrugged. 'I can control a hacking pony, at any rate,' she asserted drily, knowing stables only hired out their more docile animals.

'All right, if you'll take him, I'd be grateful.' His tone was formal rather than warm, but she felt he meant what he said. 'The stables are on the far side of Oxford, so you'll need to take a taxi.'

'That'll cost a fortune,' Clare protested without thinking. 'I'm sure there must be a bus——'

'Forget it,' he dismissed. 'I suspect you'll need all your patience with Miles at the stables. I wouldn't use it up on public transport, before you even get there.'

'All right.' Clare decided not to argue the point. Perhaps Miles might choose to be difficult if he didn't like her substituting for his father.

He certainly complained later in the taxi, saying, 'I suppose he couldn't be bothered coming.'

'It wasn't a question of not bothering,' Clare declared shortly. 'He has business, as he said.'

'Oh, yeah!' The boy wore his best sceptical look—the one he'd learned from his father. 'Is that what he told you? Well, did you see that red car that we almost banged into when we came out of the drive?'

Clare nodded. She vaguely remembered the car, although not the driver.

'Well, that was Professor Millar,' he announced with a dramatic air.

'So?' Clare had missed the point. 'Who's he?'

'Not he—*she*.' Miles pulled a face. 'The one I told you about.'

'Oh!' Clare remembered now—the girlfriend. It was a moment before she made the connection. A history professor, Ms Millar must also be the governor of Miles's prospective school. Presumably she was going to support his application. 'I believe his business concerns her,' she added for Miles's benefit.

'Business, huh!' Miles showed a cynicism beyond his years. 'Maybe I should wise you up about dear old Rosalind, because chances are she'll be bossing you about, too, if she gets him to marry her.'

'Oh,' Clare murmured inadequately as her heart sank at this news.

'I'm not making it up,' Miles added, unsure how to read her silence. 'She hasn't been around because she's spent the summer doing research at Harvard, in America.

That's her idea of a holiday!' He screwed up his face in disgust. 'Anyway, you won't like her. Nobody does.'

'Miles!' Clare reproved, and felt obliged to point out, 'Don't you think you're being rather extreme? Your father must like her, for a start.'

'Well, Aunt Lou doesn't,' he countered to support his argument. 'I heard her say so. She thinks she's too much a blue sock for him.'

'Blue stocking,' Clare corrected automatically, knowing she should stop the conversation there.

But she let Miles continue, 'Something like that . . . I mean, she talks like a walking encyclopaedia—real mega-bore stuff.'

'Miles——' Clare tried to quell him.

'Just wait and see.' He pulled another face. 'Wait till she starts telling you what to do. See how long you stick around,' he added grimly.

Clare kept her expression blank, hiding the real consternation she felt. She hadn't considered how a new mistress would affect her, and, now that she did, she hated the idea.

She had to admit that, as a boss, Fen was ideal. He never questioned what she cooked, never criticised how she cleaned. She presented him with weekly accounts and he accepted them without comment. He rarely made her feel like a servant, so she could live with being one.

But things would change under new management. A mistress of the house would want things run her way. She was bound to issue more orders. Clare wasn't sure if her pride would allow her to take them.

As a girl, she had watched helplessly the way the Holsteads had treated her mother. In front of her guests Lady Abbotsford had called Mary Anderson a 'treasure' but, in the privacy of the kitchens, she had talked to her as if she were a slave. Her mother had put up with it because she'd had a child to raise, but Clare had no such restraints. Common sense might dictate that she hold on to her job, but would it help her keep her temper?

Miles realised he'd worried her and tried to make up for it. 'It's OK. She won't sack you. She can't cook, and she thinks too much of herself to clean, so Dad'll still need you.'

Clare smiled weakly at the boy's reassurance. She didn't fool herself, however. His dad needed *someone* to cook and clean. He didn't need *her*. She understood the distinction.

'I won't *let* her sack you,' Miles added, his handsome face set in stubborn lines.

Clare was touched at his show of loyalty, and forced another smile, saying, 'Let's not waste time worrying about what might happen... Let's just concentrate on today. What do you think our horses will be like?' she asked as a distraction.

'Dog food,' Miles declared with offhand contempt. 'They usually are at stables.'

'Possibly,' Clare agreed, knowing that they were unlikely to be given thoroughbreds for a casual ride, 'but it should still be fun. It's years since I've ridden.'

'Oh, well, don't worry, I'll show you what to do,' Miles offered generously.

'Good.' Clare hid a smile, doubting she would need his help.

The Holsteads had always kept racing stables, and successfully bred several champions. As a youngster, she had run errands and mucked out stables and brushed coats to a silken sheen just to be allowed to ride one day. She had progressed from the hacks that the Holstead children had discarded to exercising the brood mares, to finally acting temporary jockey to the racers due for sale. Horses had been her grand passion before Johnny Holstead had first noticed her.

Now her thoughts strayed involuntarily to Johnny. He'd been dark-haired and brown-eyed, a handsome boy not yet a man, the summer they'd spent together. She recalled the last time she'd seen him—the last time anyone had seen him. He'd still been attractive, although too much hard living was beginning to take its toll.

She hadn't loved him for a long time. By then, she hadn't even liked him very much—but she hadn't killed him, either...

CHAPTER SEVEN

'SORRY, Miles?' Her attention returned to the boy as he tugged at her sleeve.

'We're here,' he announced as they turned off the main road into woodland and drove along a tarred track for a mile or two. At the end was a large house with stables attached.

It was mid-morning and the sun was already high in the sky, promising a cloudless day. The man in charge of the riding centre enquired about their experience and, deciding neither was a complete novice, gave them two reasonable horses. The riding centre was situated in the middle of a national park and the bridle-paths were clearly marked among the woodland.

They were allowed to go riding without supervision. Much of the way they had to walk their horses but sometimes they could get up to a canter in the clearer parts of the wood. Clare had forgotten how much she enjoyed riding; it seemed like a lifetime ago since it had been her main obsession.

They rode for a couple of hours until the sun was overhead and they felt their shirts begin to stick to their backs, then they returned to the centre for lunch at the café near by.

That was where Fen found them. He had promised to pick them up at one-thirty but it was nearer two o'clock when he arrived. Clare hadn't told Miles he was expected in case he failed to turn up for any reason.

'Dad!' Miles's face broke into a grin. 'You've come. That's terrific. You can come out with us now.'

'Like this?' Fen's tone was more amused than sarcastic as he indicated his clothing. He had discarded jacket and tie, but still wore a white shirt and tailored suit trousers.

'I suppose you'd look a bit funny,' Miles conceded, 'but we wouldn't mind. Would we, Clare?'

'No, not at all,' Clare managed to say with a straight face.

'Well, that's big of the two of you,' Fen responded, a smile in his voice.

'Great!' Miles took the comment as agreement and ran on, 'Will I go see if they have a horse big enough for you?'

'No, I think I'll do that for myself,' his father asserted drily. 'I don't fancy being landed with a Shetland pony.'

He raised his eyes towards Clare, before going to make arrangements. She tried to imagine him on the back of a pony. At six two, his feet would probably trail on the ground.

In fact she thought he'd look an unlikely character on any horse, but she was wrong. The stable gave him a huge black horse with a hint of belligerence in his eye, and, with sleeves rolled up, hard hat on, and back straight in the saddle, Fen somehow managed to look the part.

His horse, however, still had his doubts, and the moment they were away from the centre and on the bridle-path he started a skittish dance of protest. Miles was already ahead but Clare watched rather worriedly as Fen tried to subdue the animal. It took some strong handling on the reins before the horse accepted who was boss.

'Don't worry.' Fen read the doubts on her face. 'I may not be in line for a Horseman of the Year award, but I should just about be able to stay on.'

'You're doing fine.' Clare meant to give encouragement.

'Liar.' He laughed without force. 'It's a lifetime since I've been on a horse, and it shows.'

A lifetime. It was an echo of Clare's own thoughts. She supposed his life, like hers—like most people's—fell into distinct time zones. She wondered when he had ridden—as a boy or a man. Maybe with his wife. Did her interest in polo-players extend to an interest in horses?

'My father kept horses for hunting,' he answered her unspoken thoughts. 'He insisted I learn to ride, but I never saw the point of chasing a helpless animal for miles just so a pack of other animals could kill it.'

'Hear! Hear!' Clare supported his view whole-heartedly. She'd always deplored hunting.

He inclined his head and murmured, 'Well, it's nice to have your approval for something, Miss Anderson.'

His 'Miss Anderson' was said tongue-in-cheek. His smile said more.

Clare felt a blush creeping up her cheeks and changed the subject, saying, 'Miles is a good rider.'

'Very,' he agreed, as they both watched the boy a little ahead. 'I've considered buying him a horse of his own. Perhaps I will now he's remaining at home.'

'You got him a place?' Clare concluded, not hiding her pleasure.

He nodded. 'After suitably humbling myself. Like all headmasters, he wanted me to appreciate the honour he was bestowing me in allowing my child to come to Arnold's. The fact that I'm paying for the privilege is irrelevant.'

'Did Professor Millar help?' Clare had asked before she could stop herself.

He glanced at her, eyebrows raised slightly. 'Yes, Mrs Millar put in a word on my behalf. I suppose Miles told you about her.'

'He mentioned her in passing,' Clare admitted vaguely.

'I can imagine,' he returned drily, but did not expand on it.

Clare was left wondering what place the woman did occupy in his life. He obviously didn't want to discuss

her, as he suggested instead that they pick up their pace
to catch up Miles who had cantered ahead.

The wood had cleared to open land, but Clare was
still nervous for Fen. She rode ahead of him, but kept
turning to check that he was still in the saddle. She need
not have worried. He turned out to be competent enough.

'Will I pass?' he asked, when they eventually slowed
back to a walking pace.

Clare hadn't realised she'd been so obvious. 'With a
little practice,' she threw back a little cheekily.

He just laughed. 'Riding was never one of my major
talents. You look fairly impressive, however.'

'Thank you.' Clare smiled at what sounded like a
genuine compliment.

'Did you ride competitively?' he pursued.

She shook her head. 'I never had my own horse.'

'Oh, yes, you worked at a racing stables,' he recalled.
'To whom did they belong?'

'I—um—can't remember,' Clare said rather than lie.

He wasn't fooled. 'Or don't want to?' he suggested
astutely.

'Perhaps,' she admitted, then gave a dismissive shrug.
'It was a long time ago.'

'Fair enough,' he said, and moved on to talk of other
things.

Clare was grateful. Arguably he had a right to know
her past. She was looking after his child. Yet he seemed
to accept her right to privacy. Or was he just not
interested?

His lack of curiosity was marked but then housekeepers probably didn't rate his attention, and she was
one of many.

'Remember your place'—that had been one of her
mother's favourite phrases when she'd been young and
sometimes over-familiar with the Holstead children.

She tried to do that now, but Fen made it difficult.
They rode abreast, with Miles blazing the trail ahead,

and Fen talked to her as if she was simply his companion, a friend.

Relaxed, Fen Marchand was a different man from the one she'd first met. He made her smile, laugh, feel good about herself. She was beginning to like him—like him too much.

When they returned to the stables, he dismounted first, and reached up to her. She was already half off the saddle and he gave her no choice. His hands on her waist, he lifted her to the ground. His hands lingered for a moment, firm, strong hands almost spanning her slim frame.

'You've caught the sun,' he said, his eyes resting on her face.

'I—I...' Clare knew her cheeks were burning and wondered if she looked as hot and dishevelled as she felt.

She took a step away from him, and winced a little at a twinge of pain in her back.

He noted her expression, saying, 'Stiff?'

'As a board,' she confirmed, her bones already protesting at a day in the saddle.

'You'll have to have a long soak in the bath,' he suggested, his gaze running down her length as if assessing the damage, before returning to her face.

His eyes were a very distinct blue. She'd always thought them cold. They weren't now, as they looked at her.

Clare found herself thinking all kind of things she shouldn't, and pointed out, 'Miles needs your help.'

He smiled a little, amused by his own thoughts, before taking the hint and going to help Miles down.

Clare was left wondering if Dr Fenwick Marchand, M.A. Ph.D., Professor of Political History, Oxford University, et cetera, et cetera, had actually just been flirting with her.

She told herself not to be a fool, but when they went to the car and he operated the remote unlocking device he said to Miles, 'Let Clare sit in the front.'

'Sure.' Miles grinned, looking oddly pleased about something.

'No, it's all right.' Clare made a positive dive for the back seat. 'I'll be more comfortable here.'

Fen raised a brow of disbelief but didn't argue the matter, and, with the boy joining him in the front, took the opportunity to tell him of his new school.

Miles didn't hide his delight, turning to Clare to say, 'Thanks,' as he assumed she'd intervened on his behalf.

'I didn't do anything,' Clare denied. 'It was your father's idea.'

The boy turned back to his father. 'Thanks, Dad.'

'I didn't do that much, either.' His father followed Clare's suit. 'If you have to thank anyone, it's Professor Millar. She used her influence as a governor of Arnold's.'

'Oh.' The single sound suggested that Miles would sooner thank just about anyone else.

'So, I expect you to be suitably grateful,' his father went on, 'when she comes to dinner tonight.'

'She's coming to dinner?' Miles didn't disguise his despair at the idea.

Clare might have echoed his words. It was all news to her.

Fen caught her less than pleased look in the mirror and said, 'Sorry, I meant to say earlier. If it's a problem, we'll go out somewhere.'

'No, I can manage.' Clare told herself that a good housekeeper could always arrange a dinner party at three hours' notice—and keep her thoughts and feelings to herself.

But, later, as she prepared dinner, she found herself wondering what Rosalind Millar was like. Different from his wife, she assumed. From Miles's description and the facts, she'd been a spoilt, careless woman who'd thought of herself and the moment and no further. Clare couldn't imagine Fen doing anything he hadn't calculated from all angles, but it seemed his marriage had been an impulse thing, an attraction of opposites that had led ultimately to disaster.

Well, it wouldn't be a problem with Rosalind Millar, Clare thought later when she met the woman who was main candidate for Mrs Marchand the second. Crisply smart in a green linen dress, she was stylish without being flamboyant. Her black hair was arranged in a perfect chignon, without an errant wisp, and framed a high-cheeked, intelligent face that was undeniably attractive. She wore just the right amount of jewellery to give a touch of femininity and the right amount of make-up for a dinner *en famille*. She exuded the competence of a thirty-something career woman who was in charge of her life, and was, to all intents and purposes, ideal for Fen Marchand.

Clare disliked her on sight.

Perhaps it was all that self-confidence, or maybe Miles had already planted the seeds of prejudice, Clare wasn't sure, but her hackles went up the first time the woman spoke.

'You must be Clare.' The older woman smiled briefly as Clare arrived with the starters. 'Ah, smoked salmon—Scottish or Norwegian?' she enquired. 'Scottish, I'd venture, by the colour.'

'Norwegian,' Clare found herself lying purposely.

'Really?' A finely pencilled brow went up. 'Still, some people say it's as good. Have you tried it with asparagus tips? Delicious!'

Clare concluded that the woman wasn't addressing her, but she still took it as a form of criticism. The fish was the wrong nationality, the celery the wrong vegetable.

'Aren't you having any, Miles?' Rosalind Millar enquired pleasantly enough.

'Don't like it,' Miles muttered, then exchanged an almost secret smile with Clare as she served him his favourite—melon and prawn balls.

'You might if you tried it,' she suggested, steel behind her smile.

'Or I might throw up,' Miles threatened in return.

'Miles.' His father shot him a warning look, but then seemed to take his side. 'I'm afraid Miles has been allowed to eat pretty much what he wanted in the past.'

'Of course, poor boy.' Rosalind Millar awarded Miles an appropriate look of pity for the years he'd spent with his mother and grandfather.

Clare caught it as she made for the door, and thought it was the most phoney expression she'd ever seen. She wondered if Miles would last the dinner without an explosion.

It must have been the relief of no boarding-school that kept him in his seat because, by the time Clare came to clear plates and serve the next course, he had sunk into a sullen silence. Rosalind Millar had obviously given up trying to engage him in conversation and was talking of Harvard, where she'd spent part of her holiday.

Clare couldn't help listening as she served the meat course. She had to admit that the woman was an interesting conversationalist as she talked of the differences between American and English colleges. Fenwick listened intently, too, barely aware of Clare as she whipped away his dirty plate. He obviously regarded Rosalind Millar as very intelligent company. That was possibly because she was.

But she was also master of the subtle put-down, as she revealed when she finished the anecdote she was telling and noticed the main course.

'Ah, *boeuf bourguignon*—it smells delicious,' she gave Clare credit for the meal, then immediately took it away as she said to Fenwick, 'Red meat is almost like forbidden fruit these days. Since all the propaganda on healthy eating, I've been sticking religiously to fish and chicken . . . Still, I don't suppose one meal will clog up my arteries,' she laughed up at Clare.

Clare didn't laugh back. Fenwick had sprung this dinner on her at the last minute and she had spent the last two hours slaving in the kitchen. She didn't need to hear how her choice of meals was going to contribute to them all having heart attacks.

Perhaps Fenwick recognised the mutinous look on her face, because once more he stepped in. 'I must admit I don't have to worry on that score. Clare is a very varied cook and provides us with what I'm sure is a balanced diet.'

'Yes, of course.' The woman smiled condescendingly at Clare. 'I'm afraid I'm not much one for the culinary arts. Where did you learn your skills, Clare? College?'

'No,' Clare responded flatly, and had no inclination to give away more. What cooking skills she had had been acquired hanging round the kitchens of the Holstead family, helping out the cook and maid at her mother's request.

Her reluctance was noted by Rosalind Millar. 'Oh, I'm sorry. I should have thought. Did you do it—um—inside?' she asked, as if it was a delicate question.

Clare felt a moment's pain at *his* betrayal. It was naïve of her. Of course he'd tell his girlfriend about her background.

'In prison, I mean,' the woman persisted at her silence.

'No, I didn't cook in prison,' Clare stated with deliberate bluntness. 'I worked in the library.'

'Really? How fascinating,' Rosalind Millar commented with feigned interest. 'Did you get to order books or simply collate them?'

'There was already a fairly good selection,' Clare responded, 'but sometimes, if funds were available, we'd canvass opinion on what to purchase.'

'I see.' The condescending smile returned. 'I suppose most requests were for romantic novels.'

'Yes,' Clare agreed, then dared to continue, 'I don't see what's wrong with that. They mightn't be very educational but they cheer people up.'

'Literary Valium, you mean,' Rosalind Millar summed up, and gave a dry, sarcastic laugh. 'Still, it's a pity inmates can't use their time more productively—in study, for instance. Didn't they offer you any vocational courses?' she went on to enquire, as Clare placed the choice of vegetables on serving-mats.

'I did three A levels,' Clare found herself admitting, 'English, history and psychology.'

Fenwick Marchand raised a surprised brow from the end of the table. He'd obviously considered her totally uneducated, and had said as much to his girlfriend, along with discussing her prison origins, of course.

'I *am* impressed,' Rosalind Millar said, not meaning a word. With a doctorate in history, she'd hardly rate school-level qualifications. 'Did you pass?'

'I got two As and a B,' Clare stated factually before directing at Fenwick in her best servant's voice, 'Will that be all, sir?'

'Yes, Clare, that will be all,' he repeated heavily, his eyes reflecting annoyance at her tone.

She walked towards the door and, before she closed it behind her, heard Rosalind Millar laugh and say, 'Funny little thing, isn't she? Do you really think she has three A levels?'

She didn't wait to hear his answer. No doubt he thought it unlikely, too, that she had any qualifications.

Well, what did she care? Clare asked herself. He was welcome to Rosalind Millar and she to him, as long as it didn't affect her.

But it would, Clare realised later, when she brought coffee to the living-room and found Rosalind Millar on her own for a moment.

'Just put it there.' The older woman indicated the table, and, before Clare could disappear, added, 'Fen's

looking for some papers in his study so perhaps you and
I can have a quick word.'

'About what?' Clare frowned.

'Well, correct me if I'm wrong——' Rosalind gave her
a thin smile '—but I sense a certain hostility in your
attitude.'

The woman waited to be contradicted. Clare remained silent.

'And I just want to reassure you,' she continued superciliously, 'that, should my relationship with Fenwick
progress to something of a permanent nature, your job
is in no way vulnerable. Even if I had the time to indulge
in the culinary arts, I certainly don't have the inclination... I trust you understand me?'

'I think so,' Clare said in a tone that suggested she
was slow-witted, then proved she wasn't by adding, 'You
mean if Mr Marchand marries you I won't be sacked
because you can't be bothered doing the cooking.'

'I...' For once Rosalind Millar was speechless, unable
to deal with Clare's directness. 'Well, really!' she finally
managed. 'I don't know——'

'No, you don't!' Clare dismissed rather rudely, and,
before she was tempted to say more, turned on her heel.
It was then that she discovered Fen in the doorway. How
much had he heard?

Most of it, she guessed as his eyes caught and held
hers. She stared back, not about to apologise. What
would be the point? He would decide for himself if she'd
committed the unforgivable.

His eyes narrowed as she returned his stare and he
muttered, 'I'll see you later.'

'Yes, sir,' she said, and gave the faintest bob of a
curtsy.

His mouth set in an even thinner line, noting the insolence. He chose to ignore it, however, as he dismissed
her with the slight flick of his head and crossed to join
the other woman. Clare walked out of the door, but this

time left it slightly ajar and deliberately eavesdropped in the corridor.

'Fenwick,' she heard Rosalind Millar try to cover her embarrassment, 'I must say what a peculiar girl that is. I just asked her if she was settled here, and the next moment she was demanding to know if I planned to marry you and sack her,' she recounted with a superior laugh that suggested the whole thing had been Clare's fantasy.

'Yes, I suppose she is peculiar,' Fenwick agreed in an almost offhand manner, before changing the subject by enquiring, 'I must thank you again for helping Miles gain a place at Thomas Arnold's. Where do you——?'

Peculiar, was she? Clare seethed her way to the kitchen as she thought of how cleverly Rosalind Millar had twisted things and how easily Fenwick had been deceived. Perhaps they deserved each other, however unwelcome the idea. If Rosalind Millar was set to become Rosalind Marchand, would Clare really want to work for such a woman?

Maybe the choice wouldn't be hers, she realised as Fenwick approached her later. She was just on her way to bed when he caught her on the stairs.

'Miss Anderson,' he said with studied formality, 'I'd like a word.'

He turned and went back to the living-room. She was left to walk back downstairs and follow him. She assumed she was going to be carpeted in front of the brilliant Mrs Millar, but there was no sign of the woman. She must have left while Clare was cleaning up the kitchen.

Fenwick stood by the fireplace and did not invite Clare to sit, before launching in with, 'Perhaps you'd like to tell me what you were discussing with Mrs Millar earlier.'

'I...we weren't *discussing* anything,' Clare denied with emphasis. 'Mrs Millar merely informed me of her intentions and I confirmed my understanding.'

She echoed the other woman's pedantic way of talking.
It was noted.

'I believe I caught your "confirmation",' he responded drily. 'What I wish to know is what prompted
you to be so rude... Did Mrs Millar suggest our marriage was imminent?'

In truth, Clare couldn't claim she had. She had merely
hinted at their relationship becoming permanent.

'No,' she admitted heavily.

'Have I suggested as much?' he pursued.

'No,' she admitted again, wishing now she'd kept her
mouth shut earlier.

'I see, so you've decided my intentions all by yourself,'
he said with deadly dry sarcasm. 'So, presumably you
think Mrs Millar and I are a suitable match?' His voice
lifted, making it a question. A silence followed while he
waited for Clare's answer. What did he want her to say?

'I... it's none of my business,' Clare reverted to her
usual defence.

'No, it isn't,' he agreed, 'but that doesn't often prevent
you airing an opinion. So, please, feel free——' He inclined his dark blond head in invitation.

Clare knew this sarcasm was intended to put her in
her place, and she struggled to accept it. But she was
still smarting from being deemed 'peculiar'.

'Actually, yes,' she finally answered, straight-faced,
'I think you're *very* much suited to each other.'

On the face of it her reply couldn't be faulted, or her
tone. But Fenwick Marchand was no fool, and he
drawled back, 'I realise there's an insult in there. I just
wonder if I should bother looking for it.'

Clare's mouth twisted, but she said nothing. She'd
already said enough, without really saying anything.

'I take it you didn't like Mrs Millar.' He surprised her
with his directness.

She shrugged. 'Are my feelings relevant?'

'They might be,' he suggested, 'If I *were* to marry
Rosalind and you had to take orders from her.'

She felt his eyes resting on her face, waiting for her reaction. She was careful not to betray her feelings. She had difficulty believing herself how angry she felt at the prospect of him marrying Rosalind Millar. It wasn't just worry over her livelihood or horror at being in the other woman's employ—and hence at her mercy. It was anger that he would take the easy option of marrying such a woman, when...

When what? Clare asked herself what alternative she would have him choose, but didn't allow herself to answer the question. Instead she hardened her heart.

Let him marry her. Why not? They were both clever, precise, boring people, both dead from the neck downwards. It was a match made in heaven!

'I'll take orders from her,' she agreed without a flicker of feeling, then said in a businesslike voice, 'Is it to be a small private wedding? Because if it is, do you wish me to cater for it?'

'No, I damn well don't wish you to cater for it!' he exploded back at her, dropping his air of indifference.

Clare felt a moment's fear and decided retreat was called for.

'Very well. Goodnight, sir,' she said like the good servant she wasn't, and hastily made for the exit.

He caught her on the stairs and, grabbing her arm, pulled her around. 'Don't give me that "sir" rubbish!' he growled at her.

'Let me go!' she spat back, failing to pull free.

He shifted his grip to her wrist and held her fast. 'Not till we get a few things straight. For a start, there's going to be no wedding. Not to Rosalind or anyone else. Which is just as well for you, because no woman would tolerate a lippy ex-gaolbird housekeeper with a superiority complex.'

'I—you——' Clare couldn't contain her indignation. 'That's not bloody fair. You don't know what your stuck-up piece of skirt said to me,' she retorted, slipping into the language of her fellow inmates.

'*That* . . . "piece . . . of . . . skirt",' he bit out each word deliberately, 'happens to have a doctorate in ancient history, and, as my guest, she can say what the hell she likes to you!'

'Because I'm just a servant?' Clare flared back at him, her face inches from his. 'Or because I'm an ex-con?'

'Either would do!' he snarled at her, and caught her other arm before she could think of slapping him.

'Get your hands off me!' she almost shouted at him, and didn't wait for a response as she kicked out at him.

It was a stupid thing to do, considering she'd been standing on the fifth or sixth step. He managed to avoid the blow but kept his grip on her arms. She lost her footing and her balance, and fell backwards, taking him with her. They slipped down a couple of steps, then ended up in an undignified heap on the stairs.

His weight trapped her for a moment or two and Clare felt a heat spread through her own body, even as she pushed at his shoulders, crying out, 'Get off!'

'Stop panicking!' he clipped back as he extricated himself. 'You're the one who pulled me on top of you, remember!' he pointed out, sitting on the step beside her.

'You don't think——' Clare broke off, her face flushed.

'That you were trying to seduce me?' he finished for her, and laughed harshly. 'No, even you must employ more subtle methods . . . That's assuming you bother.'

'What do you mean?' Clare challenged, angry again and forgetting the oddity of their situation, as they sat side by side on the stairs.

He turned to catch her haughty look. 'I imagine you expect your men to do the running . . . Don't you?'

'I—I have no men.' Clare detected a change in him, and was nervous of it.

'I find that hard to believe.' His eyes rested on her face, as if he might read the truth there. 'You're over-thin and your hair is too short, but it is a beautiful colour. Did you ever wear it long?'

She nodded automatically, recalling a time when her hair had flown down her back. She'd cut it two weeks after Peter's death. She'd kept it short ever since.

'And your eyes, I've never seen eyes so green.' He held her gaze with his but she refused to let him see inside her head. 'The colour of jade, and as hard as glass... You feel anger and you feel pride, but do you ever feel anything else, Clare Anderson?'

Clare shut her eyes, closing off her soul to him, and made to rise, to get away from his intrusive stare. He caught her arm once more. 'What do you want of me?' she asked tensely.

He shook his head. 'I don't know... You walk round my house like a silent shadow, yet all the time I'm aware of you.'

'Do you want me to go?' Clare asked in a quiet voice, and found herself praying that he would say no.

Instead he asked, 'Do you have anywhere to go?'

Clare was honest. She shook her head.

'You have no family?'

She shook her head again.

'Then you'd better stay,' he concluded, his face completely serious.

Relief made Clare even more honest. 'Look, I'm sorry about earlier—with Mrs Millar. I was angry that you'd told her.'

'Told her what?' He frowned for a moment, then concluded for himself. 'That you'd been in prison?' At her nod, he continued quietly, 'I didn't, not directly. I confided in a colleague when you first started. I can only assume he told Ros Millar.'

'Oh.' Clare believed him and felt a little better.

'Sorry, I should have been more discreet,' he said, his tone genuinely apologetic, then, making a slight face, he pushed off the discomfort of the step and rose to his feet.

He offered her a hand. She took it. Her fingers felt small and cold in the warmth of his. She stood on the step above him, but she still had to tilt her head to look up at him.

He held her gaze once more. His eyes were an intense blue, his brows straight and dark despite his blond colouring. His mouth, when it wasn't a line of disapproval, was surprisingly sensual. She felt the power of his attraction and a familiar weakness spread from deep within her.

She shook her head, but couldn't seem to get the words out, as his hands gently clasped her upper arms. She saw his head lower towards hers and she looked away. His lips grazed her forehead, then slowly sought her mouth.

'No.' It was a whisper on her breath as she felt the whisper of his.

He ignored it. She let him. His mouth was on hers, warm and hard, but gentle. She wanted it. She trembled and he gathered her to him. He kissed her harder and desire curled in her stomach. He pulled her closer, and she felt her body shaking as his hand pressed her hips to his. She wanted to cry out but her mouth was covered. She opened her lips and felt dizzy at the taste of him on her tongue, the smell of him in her head, the strength of him holding her.

She clutched at his shoulders, her fingers sliding over the silk of his shirt, and tried to find the will to push him away. She gasped for breath and his lips released hers, only to find the racing pulse at her neck. She felt herself losing reality, wanting this man's arms round her, pressing herself to him, pressing her lips to his rough male skin.

'Come upstairs,' he urged in a voice hoarse with emotion. 'I need you. We need each other.'

Clare shook her head, denying it. She didn't need him. She needed no one. This was just a moment of weakness.

It took all her will-power to break free—to evade the mouth seeking hers once more, to push at his chest, to cry out, 'No, *don't*!'

He let her go. He cursed harshly but he let her go. They stood on the stairs, breathing hard, their eyes locked in an ageless battle.

She half expected him to apologise as he had before—or to laugh it off, but he didn't.

'Why?' he demanded harshly.

'You don't want *me*,' Clare answered, her voice breathless but hard. 'You want a woman. I just happen to be here.'

'You believe that?' he threw back at her, then concluded angrily, 'You don't think much of me, do you?'

'No, I just think more of myself,' she retorted, her eyes as hard as glass.

This time he did laugh, a harsh, unpleasant sound. 'So you're too good for me—the princess of Pentonville?' he scoffed.

Clare didn't allow herself to crack. 'That's a male prison,' she informed him contemptuously, 'but you're getting the idea ... Stick to Rosalind Millar.'

She turned on her heel, and began to walk up the stairs. He called after her, 'Don't worry, I will.' She kept walking.

When she reached her room, she didn't cry as she had last time. She felt too furious, with herself as well as him. She didn't need him, but she had wanted him. Not any man. Just him. She didn't know why.

It wasn't love. She wasn't capable of love any more. But she admitted that she felt for him an attraction that she couldn't seem to control. It wasn't just his looks although he was very handsome, with his straight classical features offset by the hint of a cleft in his chin. Could it be the surprise of it—that underneath his dry, academic manner lay a man of anger and passion that was perhaps truer to his soul?

Was this the man Diana Marchand had married, only to find herself living with someone else?

Clare shook her head, trying to rid herself of such thoughts. It didn't matter why the marriage had broken down. Fenwick Marchand wasn't for her, would never be for her.

She could go to his bed, and sleep with him that night, or a thousand nights—it would make no difference. If he ever married again, it wouldn't be to someone like her.

Clare just had to remember that, and keep remembering it. She just had to recall how it had felt the last time her heart was broken. Simple, really.

CHAPTER EIGHT

THIS time there was no apology. He arrived for breakfast with Miles as if nothing had happened. He stared her straight in the eye, and she stared right back. Then they carried on as normal. They understood each other now.

She didn't suggest leaving. That would mean running away, because she didn't trust herself. She wouldn't give him the satisfaction. Let him sack her if he couldn't live with it.

It seemed he could, however. He obviously had no plans to replace her. Her driving lessons continued and she knew he hadn't simply forgotten about them. She saw him watching her leave with Paul Dyson, her instructor.

She supposed he needed her for Miles's sake, to run and collect him from school. Nor did she feel she could let the boy down, especially as he was so supportive of her.

He approached her the day after the dinner with Rosalind Millar, and asked her directly, 'Clare, have you really been to prison?'

Clare nodded.

'What for?' the boy pursued.

'Stealing,' she confessed quietly.

'Oh.' The boy struggled to come to terms with what he knew of Clare and what he had just discovered. 'I bet you had a good reason.'

'I *thought* I had,' Clare corrected carefully, 'but it just made things worse. Honesty really is the best policy.'

Miles nodded in agreement. 'Any time I lie, Dad finds out, and then he flips. He hates that sort of thing. It's because he's so straight himself.'

Clare supposed Fen Marchand was. He'd proved himself a fair employer. He'd also been brutally honest about his feelings for her; he'd wanted her, he'd even admitted to sexual need, but he'd not once pretended any love or liking for her.

'I suppose that's why Aunt Lou asked Dad to give you a chance,' Miles recalled. 'Were you just out of gaol?'

'Yes,' Clare admitted.

Miles considered the matter further before declaring, 'I don't think Dad should have told Mrs Millar. It isn't her business.'

Clare might have agreed, but said instead, 'Perhaps he thinks she should know.'

'If they get married, you mean,' Miles concluded gloomily.

'Possibly.' Clare decided not to tell Miles that his father had denied any intention of marrying. He wouldn't be the first man to say one thing and do another where marriage was concerned.

Certainly he seemed to take her advice and turned all his attention to Rosalind Millar. While Clare stopped dining with the family, the other woman seemed to appear every other day at the house for lunch or dinner.

On one of these occasions she wandered into the kitchen. Clare had just given Miles some lemonade and a chocolate biscuit.

'Ah, Miles, there you are... What are you drinking?' she asked in freezing tones.

'I—um—it's lemonade.' Miles was puzzled as to what he'd done wrong.

'Well, you can stop drinking it this second,' she informed him coldly, then turned on Clare. 'I don't suppose you know much about nutrition, with your background, but I would be grateful if you don't feed the child on junk.'

'It's just a small glass of lemonade,' Clare said in a tone that told the other woman she was over-reacting.

'And a big dose of preservatives, colourants and God knows what else,' Rosalind Millar claimed stridently.

Clare always bought the brand that boasted no preservatives and such like, but she saw no point in saying so.

'Nor would I allow him to eat biscuits all day,' the other woman continued with a superior air. 'No wonder he's...hyperactive.'

'Miles isn't hyperactive.' Clare wasn't willing to let such rubbish pass. She mightn't be a history professor but she had studied a bit of child psychology on her A level course, and Miles showed no sign of such a condition.

'Oh, and what makes you a child expert?' Rosalind Millar visibly sniffed with disdain. 'Don't tell me. You read all about it in some women's magazine... Well, I think I'd sooner have the opinion of a trained clinical psychologist.'

She really was good at the put-down. Clare, mindful of her position in the household, was left counting to ten.

It was Miles who spoke up, stating almost matter-of-factly, 'Clare's right. My mother took me to a psychologist and he said I'm not hyperactive. He just charged a lot more money to say so,' he added with a very cynical touch for one so young.

Rosalind Millar breathed very loudly, while she searched for an appropriate response. Clare didn't quite manage to keep a smile off her face, and Miles openly grinned. It was the two of them against the world.

Rosalind Millar must have realised as much as she looked from one to the other. 'I wonder if Fenwick is aware of the influence you have over his son?' From her expression, she clearly didn't consider it a good influence. 'Perhaps it's time someone told him,' she added, a last threat as she backed out of the room.

Miles pulled a face the moment she disappeared. 'Boy, I can't believe Dad's really serious about her.'

'Miles,' Clare half-heartedly reproved as she too wondered how close Rosalind Millar and his father were. The woman so clearly thought she had the right to tell off both Miles and her, it suggested that their relationship was on its way to some form of permanency.

How far on its way, Clare discovered a couple of days later, when she rose to make breakfast. Miles appeared late, saying his father had failed to wake him, and ate his cereal, comic in hand. When Fen Marchand hadn't arrived at the table some twenty minutes later, she began to wonder whether he'd slept in.

She knew he'd been out to dinner, because he'd asked her specifically to babysit Miles. His car wasn't on the courtyard and the garage at the back was standing open and empty. She guessed he'd returned by taxi as he had previously—the time she'd gone looking for burglars and found him instead.

His social life was clearly picking up, Clare thought with a touch of irrational anger as she went upstairs to tidy the rooms. She did Miles's room first, then the bathroom and toilet. She left Fenwick's till last, and knocked tentatively on the door. It drew no response and she opened the door quietly, popping her head round the side.

There was no one there. Not only that, the bed was still made up from yesterday. Wherever Fen Marchand had slept, it wasn't in his own bed.

Clare's stomach went into knots, an involuntary emotion, and she backed almost violently out of the room. She backed right into someone, and let out a small cry of fright as hard male hands caught and steadied her.

'It's only me,' Fen Marchand said as she wrested out of his grip and pivoted round.

'Yes!' She almost snapped the word, inexplicably angry.

He misread it as guilt and narrowed his eyes. 'What were you doing in my room?'

'I was going to clean it,' she retorted, 'but, as it hasn't been slept in, I don't think I'll bother.'

A fraction of a tone away from open insolence, it had the man's mouth compressing into a thin line, but his anger was brief, replaced by something more speculative. 'No, you're right,' he surprised her by agreeing, 'there's no point. In fact, any time I stay out all night, you can leave my room.'

'Fine,' Clare said in a voice of ice, and made to walk away.

He moved slightly, just enough to block her exit. 'Don't you want to know where I've been?'

'Not particularly,' she said, but her eyes betrayed her feelings.

'You think I've been with Ros Millar, don't you?' he said, with more than a hint of amusement.

It made Clare feel worse. She was fighting to keep her temper, not sure why she was in danger of losing it, and he regarded the whole thing as some kind of joke.

'It's none of my business,' she declared heavily.

'Ah, your favourite response.' He arched an eyebrow. 'And, of course, you're technically right. If I want to sleep with Mrs Millar, I don't require your approval. Which is just as well, from the icy waves of *disapproval* I presently detect,' he added as Clare's face tightened even more.

'You can do what you like, for all I care,' she asserted angrily, and made to push past him.

He caught her arm. 'Look at me. Come on, look!' he ordered, and she lifted her head to meet his eyes. 'Do I look like a man who has spent the night making love?'

'I . . .' Colour rushed to Clare's cheeks at his blunt question. She didn't know how to answer it. He looked as he always did—clean-shaven, blond hair ruthlessly brushed down, faintly myopic round the eyes without his glasses. He showed no sign of fatigue; rather he looked as if he'd had a good night's sleep.

'Do I?' He demanded a response, his mouth twisting a little in mockery.

He was clearly enjoying her discomfort. The fact made Clare madder and she forgot her embarrassment, forgot their respective positions as she matched his bluntness with a rash, 'No, but I imagine Mrs Millar is just about as exciting in bed as she is out of it!'

He looked offended for a moment, as if a stray dog he'd thrown scraps to had suddenly bitten back. He hadn't expected her to retaliate in kind. But he surprised her with his reaction.

'Not as exciting as you, I bet,' he replied so quietly that she barely caught it. But she caught more clearly the look he gave her, his eyes losing their distance, focusing on her: seductive blue eyes—bedroom eyes.

For a moment she felt it, the warmth of his desire, the force of her own, and she was paralysed. Then he smiled, and she saw the amusement in his eyes, and anger freed her.

'Oh, go to hell!' she said to the man who was her employer, who gave her room and board and a hefty wage on top, and, not waiting for his response, turned tail and went back up to the corridor, heading for the sanctuary of her flat in the attic.

He didn't pursue her, but his laughter did, low and mocking, as she fled from him. He had won that round and they both knew it.

She should have left then, she recognised later. But it was hard. She had nowhere to go, and, despite her problems with him, she felt safe at Woodside Hall—at home in her little flat with the books and bric-a-brac she'd bought on her weekly trip to Oxford.

There were her driving lessons, too. Soon she would be ready to sit her test. She'd worked hard for her licence, even though she'd been less than fond of her instructor, Paul Dyson.

In his thirties and quite attractive, with dark hair and even features, he was the type of man who had a wife and children at home, but still insisted on chatting up every female in sight. So far, Clare had managed to put him off without causing too much offence.

Fen still seemed keen on her obtaining her licence, too, as he appeared in the courtyard after one of her lessons a couple of days later to speak to Dyson.

'How is she getting on?' he asked directly of the instructor.

'Very well, Mr Marchand,' Paul Dyson declared with an oily smile. 'She should be ready for her test quite soon.'

'Good.' Fenwick nodded his approval, then, without looking in Clare's direction, disappeared back inside.

'Cool customer, your boss,' Paul Dyson commented. 'How long have you worked for him?'

'A couple of months,' she responded shortly.

He wasn't discouraged. 'And what is it you do—secretarial work?'

She shook her head, and again answered briefly, 'Housekeeping.'

Paul Dyson looked surprised. 'I always imagined housekeepers were boot-faced and at least fifty...you're definitely neither.' He gave her an admiring leer.

'Really?' Clare couldn't have sounded less interested.

He still went on, 'It must be lonely for you out here, miles from Oxford. There can't be much to do, and your boss can hardly be described as a barrel of laughs.'

No, Clare agreed silently, Fenwick Marchand certainly didn't fit that description.

'I was wondering,' Dyson continued obviously, 'if you'd fancy coming out for a jar with me some time. Not in that——' He nodded at the modest Fiesta he used for instruction. 'I've got a Cosworth for my own use. We could go into Oxford, go to a club or something,' he added persuasively.

Clare wasn't remotely tempted but she said, 'All of us, you mean.'

'What?' He didn't follow.

'All of us—you, me... and your wife?' she enquired pointedly.

He betrayed himself with the merest flicker of guilt, before trying to bluff his way out of it. 'Wife? What makes you think I'm married?'

'You mean besides the lady's umbrella down here and the *Winnie the Pooh and Friends* tape there?' She nodded towards the cassette carrier. 'Absolutely nothing,' she finished with deadpan sarcasm.

He looked into her face and saw her sharp, intelligent eyes and decided to come clean. 'All right, I do have a wife, but not for long. We're getting a divorce.'

'I wonder why,' Clare said very drily, and didn't give him a chance to respond, before climbing out of the driver's side and heading towards the front door.

Paul Dyson, however, was unoffended, as he climbed out the other side and called after her, 'Should I take that as a no?'

'Emphatically,' Clare called back, and laughed a little at the nerve of him as she entered the house. She found Fenwick standing in the hall.

'What's so funny?' He glowered at her as if he'd expressly forbidden laughter in the house.

'Nothing—just a joke Paul Dyson told me,' she lied because it was easier.

'Really?' His mouth thinned, expressing distaste. 'You're on friendly terms with him?'

Clare could have denied it. She wasn't on anything approaching friendly terms with Paul Dyson. But she decided none of this was Fenwick's business, so she simply answered with a shrug. He took it as a yes.

'He's probably married, you realise,' he declared with an almost Victorian air of disapproval.

A derisive smile briefly slanted Clare's mouth. She hid it, but not soon enough.

'You find that funny, too?' he demanded stiffly.

'His being married, no,' she said, 'you lecturing me, yes. You employ me. You don't own me.'

His jaw went rigid as he controlled his temper, but Clare didn't care. Their relationship had gone beyond her curtsying politely while he dispensed orders. It was useless to pretend otherwise.

'I employ you, I can also sack you,' he eventually responded in a threat that wasn't remotely veiled.

Clare was scarcely quelled by it, agreeing, 'Yes, you can, can't you?'

She waited for a moment, returning his stare, almost inviting him to do as he suggested. One day he would sack her. Wouldn't it be better now, today, before——?

'Date Dyson and I will.' Fen Marchand's voice cut into her thoughts, its harshness telling her he meant every word.

He didn't wait for her response. He had laid down the law. She could either obey or get out. Clare was left fuming as he retreated back to his study.

What gave him the right to dictate her personal life? Nothing!

Once more she told herself she had to leave. In fact she got as far as planning where she might go, what she might do, how much she had saved. But again she put it off, her thoughts on Miles. Without realising it was happening, she had allowed him to become dependent on her for advice, support, company. She had to wait at least until he had settled at school and made friends. His need of her was bound to diminish then.

He went off to school the following Monday. Fen took him in his car. Term had yet to begin at the university and he returned home to work in his study.

It was an odd day for Clare. She was so used to having Miles as a companion, the house suddenly seemed large and empty. Fen emerged from his study only once to ask for a sandwich lunch. She brought it to him, but he barely looked up from his books. They had reverted to distant politeness. She went back to the kitchen and had her own at the table.

It took her a while to put a name to what she was feeling. She was lonely. It caught her by surprise. In prison she had never been alone, but that had been one of the worst parts. She had longed for privacy, for silence, for control of her own life. She had hated the forced intimacy of the institution and had built a wall around herself to make it tolerable. She had entered prison with no friend, and, but for Louise Carlton, had left the same way. She had not been lonely. She'd been alone and preferred it.

But now she was used to Miles, chattering, intruding, craving attention, and the silence of Woodside Hall was oppressive. It was almost a relief when Miles hurtled into the kitchen late that afternoon, and, without so much as a hello, launched an attack on his new school.

'Boy, what a bunch of dipsticks!' was his first scathing dismissal.

'The teachers or the pupils?' Clare enquired, without taking his comment too seriously.

'Both,' he snorted in reply, then confided with boyish disgust, 'Carlisle, my form teacher, has hair growing on the back of his knuckles.'

'Really?' Clare said for want of anything more appropriate.

'And in his ears—gross!' he added, pretending to gag. 'Do you know what I think?'

'No.' She wasn't sure if she wanted to know.

'I think,' he dropped his voice, 'he could be a...werewolf.'

'A werewolf?' Clare gave him a sceptical look, assuming he was joking.

But maybe he wasn't, as he added, 'Lycanthrope. I've read about them in my *Myth and Monster* book. The things to look out for are hairy arms and hands, browny yellow eyes too close together, and a deep voice. Mr

Carlisle has all of them,' he said, as if it were conclusive proof.

'Well, supposing you're right,' Clare said, tongue firmly in cheek, 'I think you'd better keep the fact to yourself.'

'Don't worry, we will,' he assured her readily enough.

'*We*?' she picked up.

'Angus Petrie—he thinks the same as me,' he relayed.

'Oh.' Clare wondered which bright spark first noticed Mr Carlisle's werewolf-like propensities. 'Angus, is he one of the dipsticks in your form?' she asked drily.

He nodded. 'But Angus isn't so bad. I mean, he seems a bit weird, but he's not really, he's just dead clever,' Miles said with patent admiration. 'He's a scholarship boy. That means he gets to go free because his folks have no money. In fact, he only has a mum and she sits around all day watching soap operas and smoking fags... Anyway, do you think he could come to tea?' he asked, while Clare was still trying to digest the rest.

'I don't know.' Clare wasn't sure how Fen would react to Angus and his "interesting" background. 'It's not really up to me, Miles.'

'You could ask Dad, though,' Miles urged, clearly keen to have the boy's company.

'Ask me what?' a voice interrupted, and they looked round to find his father in the doorway.

'I...' Miles looked at his father, then looked appealingly to Clare, before bowing out with, 'I'd better go and change.'

'What was it that Miles would have you ask?' his father repeated.

'Nothing important,' Clare dismissed, cleaning a sink that was already spotless. 'He just wondered if he could bring a friend home from school.'

'A friend?' He came to lean on the worktop beside her. 'You're serious? Miles has made a friend?'

'Yes, he has.' She wished he wouldn't make it sound like a miracle.

'Well, it's more than he told me.' He sighed in exasperation. 'He spent the car journey home convincing me Thomas Arnold's was one step up from Wormwood Scrubs...' There was a pause as Clare automatically tensed, and he realised his insensitivity. 'Sorry, I forget,' he added briefly.

'It's all right.' She tried to seem indifferent.

'No, it's not,' he said very quietly, his eyes briefly holding hers, before he ran on, 'Anyway, he definitely gave me the impression that his day was one catalogue of misery.'

'I think he was exaggerating. He seems to have made a friend, at any rate,' Clare relayed, 'and that's something.'

'I suppose,' he agreed thoughtfully, 'although I can't help wondering what Miles's taste in friends will be like.'

Clare was still wondering herself after the brief biography he'd given of Angus Petrie, but she decided to keep it to herself, saying instead, 'Could this boy come home for tea? I'd supervise them.'

'Yes, fine. Miles needs all the friends he can get,' he agreed, aware of his son's loneliness. 'I'll write a note to his mother, then drive him home with Miles one day... Which reminds me, do you think you're ready for your driving test?'

Clare shrugged, uncertain, but then nodded. 'I'll give it a try.'

'Fair enough. I'll arrange it for the earliest date possible. About Dyson...' He paused, selecting his words carefully. 'On reflection, I feel I was being somewhat Draconian. You may—er—disregard what I said.'

'Which bit exactly?' Clare was genuinely confused.

His face darkened a little, believing she was being deliberately obtuse. 'About dating him. Your private life is your own,' he stated stiffly.

'Yes,' she agreed just as stiffly.

He looked exasperated as he tried and failed to fathom her reaction. He'd thought he was being reasonable, generous even. She didn't seem in the least bit grateful.

Instead she could barely mask her irritation as she added, 'Is there anything else, *sir*?'

'No,' he responded heavily, and just managed to contain his own temper as she walked away from him and went towards the larder. He found himself following, standing at the door of the walk-in cupboard while she selected various tins and packets from the shelves. 'So, do you plan to?' he couldn't stop himself asking her.

Clare's fingers curled into the bag of sugar she was holding. She wished he would just go away. What game was he playing? One moment polite and formal, the next arrogant and impossible.

'Plan to what?' She refused to make her humiliation easy for him.

'Date Dyson,' he ground out.

'I don't know.' She shrugged, purposely lying, 'I'll have to think about it... Now you've given your *permission*,' she added in a tone that couldn't be anything but sarcastic.

'God, you're impossible!' he bit back, losing patience. 'I try my best to be fair and reasonable. I make concessions for you—more than any other housekeeper I've had. I ignore the fact that you're rude to my guests——' Her eyes flew to his, and he answered her unspoken question. 'Yes, Mrs Millar did relay details of your latest conduct. I pay you a good wage and allow you to run the house pretty much as you like. So why is it that you still manage to make me feel *you're* doing *me* the favour?' he finished on an exasperated note.

'Well, if you don't like it——' Clare began defensively.

'I know. I can sack you,' he concluded for her. 'Well, don't think I won't. You're not *that* important to me,' he muttered angrily, and, turning on his heel, left her with the threat hanging in the air.

Clare was more bewildered than worried by his choice of words. She had never considered herself in the least important to him. She had yet to believe that this job was anything but temporary. It surprised her every time they quarrelled that he didn't simply dispense with her services. It wasn't as if he hadn't already been through half a dozen housekeepers since Miles's return. So why not get rid of her?

Louise or Miles? One of them must be the reason. Perhaps he'd promised his sister to give her a three-month rather than one-month trial; in that case she only had another three weeks to go. Or was it Miles and her growing relationship with him?

Clare didn't like that idea. She didn't want to be important to Miles. She didn't want him to start counting on her. She couldn't get close to someone again.

Friends were clearly the answer, she concluded a few weeks later when he arrived home with Angus Petrie. He sought her out as usual, but only briefly, to introduce his companion, then disappeared upstairs. Later she served them up a special high tea and listened as they told each other silly jokes, abused their various teachers and groaned about acres of homework. It was a relief to see that Miles was liked for himself, albeit by a fellow misfit.

Even without the thick-lensed glasses and the furrowed brow, she would have picked Angus out as a brain. He possessed an astounding range of general knowledge, and was an odd mixture of working-class common sense and intelligent eccentricity.

Fortunately Fenwick appeared to approve of him, even after he drove the boy home and discovered his background for himself.

'What did you think of Angus?' he asked her directly after she'd served dinner and brought coffee to the lounge.

'I liked him,' she said, surprised that he'd seek her opinion.

He nodded in agreement. 'Very bright, I thought, and quite well-adjusted, considering his home environment.'

'Was it bad?' Clare had half discounted Miles's claim about Angus's background, having met the boy.

'Bloody awful.' Fenwick grimaced as he swallowed down some of the whisky he'd poured himself, 'Fifteenth floor of a tower block. Grafitti. Broken lift. Smashed windows. I went up with him. His mother wasn't there, but that's normal. She works till two in the morning. He looks after himself. The place is a pit, and he knows it. But he didn't try to make excuses.' He spoke with obvious admiration for the youngster.

'I suppose he's used to it,' Clare commented rather inadequately.

'True, but it didn't stop me wanting to drive back home with him here,' he admitted, a thread of anger in his voice, then he gave a brief, humourless laugh. 'Which is a bit of a joke, all things considered.'

'What do you mean?' Clare didn't follow.

'I'm scarcely making a resounding success of my own son's upbringing,' he admitted with surprising candour.

'That's not your fault,' she countered without thinking.

He raised a brow, obviously not expecting such support.

'He hasn't lived with you for years,' she added.

'True,' he acknowledged, 'but that was my fault. If I'd just fought harder for custody...' He shook his head, impatient with himself.

'Harder?' Clare echoed. 'In what way?'

'Dirtier,' he qualified, his mouth twisting, and, after a moment's reticence, went on to admit, 'I was too proud. I thought I could keep Miles without washing our dirty linen in public. Diana had no such qualms. By the time the custody case was over, she almost had *me* believing I was a violent alchoholic.'

'Your wife said that?' It was the last description Clare would have used for Fen Marchand. Normally he drank little, and, although she'd witnessed his temper, he'd never come near to hitting her or Miles.

'And more,' he nodded, 'but then I gave her the ammunition.'

Clare's eyes narrowed in disbelief. She forgot her role of housekeeper and pursued, 'What do you mean?'

'Not what you think.' He laughed shortly. 'To my eternal regret I never laid a hand on my dearly departed wife. However, in a less rational, less sober moment I did threaten to knock her block off,' he admitted, grimacing at his own behaviour. 'Not only that, I was stupid enough to do it with her father present. He made an excellent witness in court.'

'Why did you threaten her?' Clare dared to ask, and, at his silence, rashly added, 'Because of the other man?'

'Which one?' he retorted with bitter irony, then shook his head. 'No, by the time my wife started playing the polo field, I was well past caring... Not that she ever accepted the fact. She liked to think I was still besotted.'

His lips twisted at the memories he could see in the bottom of his now empty whisky glass. He didn't seem drunk, but Clare wondered if he might be a little. Why else would he be confiding in *her*?

'Were you... in the beginning?' she asked quietly.

He looked up from his glass to her, and frowned, as if regretting his indiscretion, but then continued, 'I suppose I must have been ... Did Lou tell you? That I married Diana six months after I met her?'

'She did say something,' Clare confirmed.

'To elicit your sympathy, no doubt,' he observed astutely. 'Lou regards my marital disaster as proof of my humanity, rather than my plain, downright stupidity. Diana and I married in haste and repented at leisure, as the saying goes. We might have parted older, wiser and a hell of a lot sooner if we hadn't had Miles.'

'Lou said your wife wasn't ready for a child,' Clare recalled, drawn into his past and feeling a need to know the truth.

'Possibly not,' he agreed, but with the attitude of a man who had thought too much over his past to make any sense of it. 'Diana liked the idea at first—believe it or not, Miles was planned. But the reality was something else. One day she'd be playing the perfect mother, the next she'd be off on her own to London for a week. The number of times she let Miles down!' he muttered with some of the anger and frustration he'd felt at the time. 'Once he was all packed up for a holiday. She showed up four days later.'

'Is that why you threatened her?' Clare guessed.

He nodded. 'Not very civilised, and incredibly stupid, as it turned out.'

'You were provoked.' Clare didn't question why she was a hundred per cent on his side. She just was.

'Perhaps.' Fen didn't seem quite so ready to forgive himself. He crossed to the drinks cabinet, then glanced at her, saying, 'Do you want...?' She shook her head and he continued, 'Tell me, do you really not drink or do you feel it might compromise your position?'

'What?' Clare blinked.

'The "me servant, you master" posture you've adopted,' he added almost casually as he poured himself another whisky and turned to face her again. 'I take it that's why you've absented yourself from dinner? Part of your no fraternisation policy.'

Clare wasn't sure if he was joking or what. There was a suggestion of a smile round his mouth, but it didn't reach his eyes.

'I assumed you wouldn't want me joining you and Professor Millar,' she clipped back, her sympathy for him rapidly disappearing.

'A fair assumption,' he conceded, 'but Mrs Millar is hardly a permanent fixture at the dining-table.'

'You could have fooled me,' Clare couldn't resist muttering under her breath.

He wasn't meant to hear it, but his eyes widened, indicating that he did. His reaction was distinctly odd, as a satisfied smile appeared on his lips.

'Anyway, I'd prefer it if you rejoined us,' he went on superciliously, 'if only to disabuse Miles of the notion that I've dumped you in favour of Mrs Millar.'

'That's ridiculous!' Clare covered her embarrassment with anger.

'Totally,' he agreed, 'but Miles has his own way of looking at things, and unfortunately he seems to have taken a dislike to Ros, whereas you can do no wrong.'

Clare assumed she was being accused of something and went on the defensive. 'I haven't been turning him against Professor Millar, if that's what you think.'

'I don't think that,' he denied almost calmly. 'Miles was against Ros from the moment they met, and that was long before you appeared in our lives. His championship of you just highlights the difference.'

'Look, that's not my fault.' Clare still felt he was attacking her, however obliquely. 'I haven't asked Miles to attach himself to me. It's just happened. He was lonely and I was there,' she concluded bluntly.

'Is that how you see things between *us*?' His eyes caught and held hers and communicated more than words, as they spoke silently of their own relationship. 'You don't have a very high opinion of yourself, do you?'

'I...it's not that.' Clare was thrown for a moment, then jumped for safer ground. 'About Miles...I'm just saying it won't last, his dependency on me. When he makes friends——'

'But what if it does last?' he cut in relentlessly.

'I...it won't,' Clare insisted. 'I mean, he's never bothered with any of your other housekeepers for long, has he?'

'No, but you're not like any of them.' He continued to stare at her. 'You're younger, prettier and a whole lot brighter. It's hardly surprising he's attached.'

Once more Clare felt she was being accused, however coolly, of something she couldn't control. She gave up being conciliatory, and threw back, 'Well, if it bothers you so much, you know what you can do——'

'Sack you?' he supplied for her. 'Yes, I can do that. Is that what you'd like?'

'*Me*?' Clare didn't see that she had any choice in the matter. 'Why should I want to be sacked?'

It was a rhetorical question but he gave it serious consideration, before speculating, 'Perhaps it isn't just a one-way street, you and Miles... you and me.'

'I don't know what you're talking about.' Clare didn't even try to work it out.

'Perhaps we're becoming a little important to you, too,' he suggested, 'and you can't cope with that.'

For a moment his perception cut through all Clare's defences. She hid the fact with anger.

'Of course you're important to me,' she responded scathingly. 'You pay my wages.'

'And that's all?' His eyes now accused her of lying. She stared back at him without any sign of emotion, a skill she'd learned in prison. He shook his head, and gave a low curse. 'God, and Lou thinks *I'm* scared of commitment...! Would it be so awful to admit a fondness of Miles, at least? I've seen the two of you together, smiling, talking, laughing. You're so natural with each other, he could be *your* son.'

'*Your* son'. The words echoed through her head. *Peter*. The name sprang to her lips, squeezed tight her heart. She held it in, but the pain was stark on her face.

Any reminder of Peter always hurt. She could go some days and only think of him once or twice; others he was there in her mind for hours.

Tears sprang to her eyes and it took all her will-power to stop them falling. She didn't want to tell Fenwick Marchand about Peter. But every moment she stood there in silence she was denying her own child, her baby.

'What's wrong?' He set his glass down, and, seeing the effect of his words, repeated, 'What is it? What's wrong?'

'I...nothing.' Clare swallowed the lump in her throat, and forced herself to act normally. 'Nothing's wrong. I...I...' She searched frantically for something to say, anything, to blank off the image of Peter in her mind.

But she was already too late. Fen Marchand wasn't stupid.

'You have a son,' he concluded in shock as he read the expression on her face.

Clare said nothing. She tried to say no. She had to, if she wanted the conversation to stop here. But she couldn't. Saying no would be the ultimate betrayal of Peter.

'Where is he?' Fen demanded.

'I...' Clare told herself to lie, and tried to, but, 'No-where... He isn't... I... He's dead,' she finally admitted, when she couldn't bring herself to do otherwise.

She shut her eyes, knowing she might cry if she didn't. She prayed Fen Marchand would leave it there. Why should he want to know of her life, her past? It meant nothing to him.

Instead he came to stand before her. 'How old?'

'I—I...' She struggled to answer him without crying. He reached out a hand, as if to touch her, and she urged, 'Please don't.'

He dropped his hand away, but repeated, 'How old?'

'Four,' she managed to breathe. 'He was four... He would have been seven next month.'

'Hell,' he swore, acknowledging the pain she must feel. 'You should have told me. Does Lou know?'

She shook her head, then said, 'No... I don't... I can't talk about it.'

'All right,' he accepted quietly, and didn't try to ask her more.

She was glad. She had to get herself out of here. She had to go, before she embarrassed them both by crying.

'I have to. . .' She backed away from him, then turned to half run from the room.

'Clare,' he called after her, but she kept going.

She ran upstairs. She heard him call her name again, but she ran on, no longer able to hold on to her feelings. She was crying before she made the second staircase up to her attic room.

She completely broke down when she reached her flat. It had been over three years since she'd cried like this for Peter. It was as if a damn had burst, pouring out her feelings in a tide of misery and loss.

Blinded by tears, she stumbled to her wardrobe and took out the cardboard box she kept there. In it was a small photograph of her son. A friend from her hotel-work days had taken it.

It was of both of them. Peter was sitting on her knee. There was little trace of her in him. Instead she saw Johnny Holstead's face staring back at her. She didn't have a picture of Johnny but she remembered well enough. He'd been boyish and handsome, weak and wild, another wasted life. She wept for him, too, as she recalled the last time she'd seen him.

He'd been just twenty-six, but he'd looked forty. His hands were shaking. His face was grey and his eyes restless. They'd been at the Holsteads' London flat when she'd given him the package, not knowing what it contained. She'd been stupid. She'd understood the rest. When she'd helped him take one of the racers from the stables and driven it to a pre-arranged spot and sold it to a cash buyer, she'd realised they were, in effect, stealing it. She had made no protest; if this was the only way she could get money, then so be it. She'd gone to London with him, as agreed, and, while he waited in the flat, she'd taken part of the money to ''debt collectors'' to whom Johnny had owed a considerable sum. They had given her a small package, and laughed when she'd asked what it was. She'd put it in her pocket and almost forgotten about it, as she'd raced back to the flat to get her "share" of the cash. Thirty thousand. Enough to fly to America with Peter and pay for treatment.

Johnny had snatched the package from her hand and disappeared to his bedroom. When he'd returned, he'd seemed better. His pallor had gone. His eyes were no longer dull, but bright and fixed. Too bright, she'd realised as he'd begun to ramble about her and Peter and the future they'd have together. Perhaps he'd meant it. Perhaps in his fevered brain he'd actually imagined they could start playing happy families. But Clare had suddenly understood what was going on.

She'd walked past him into the bedroom. The paraphernalia was on the bedside cabinet—a syringe, foil, leather strap. How stupid she'd been! All the signs had been there. She'd just not wanted to recognise them.

She'd left then, taking her money. He'd clutched at her arm, but she'd left anyway. He'd called after her, begging, but she could only hear their son's crying, small and faint, growing weaker by the day. She hadn't seen Johnny again.

He'd died later that evening. Apparently he'd been greedy—taking another fix that was too much for his system. He never woke up.

Peter had died a couple of days later in his hospital ward; he'd been too weak to travel; the money had come too late. She'd cradled his small body for an hour, then they'd taken her away.

They'd been waiting outside, two policemen and a policewoman. One would have been sufficient to arrest her. She'd gone willingly, her life over. She'd signed the confession. Yes, she'd stolen Blue Dancer, one of the Earl's best horses. Yes, she'd bought drugs with the money and given them to the Earl's son. She had not defended herself in court. She had not contradicted the lies the Holstead family had told. Their son was dead. Her son was dead. And she wanted to be dead, too.

But she'd survived. Three years in prison. She'd been attacked once, propositioned several times, and called names she'd never heard before, simply because she talked "posher" than the rest. She hadn't cried or complained, and seeing they were having no impact, the other inmates had soon left her alone. She was the only prisoner who didn't count the days to her release, the only one who never planned her life thereafter. She had no life. Her son was dead.

She cried again now, as she hadn't cried all those years in prison. She cried as if it had been just yesterday that she'd held her dying son and stroked his beautiful dark hair. She fell asleep crying, and slept deeply, drained of emotion.

She stirred a little, but did not wake when Fenwick entered her attic bedroom. He touched her hair, lightly brushing it back from her face, but she felt nothing. He covered her still clothed body with the quilt.

He watched for a while as she slept and wondered that she who seemed so strong could look so vulnerable in sleep.

He stared at the picture that had slipped from her grip, and barely recognised the girl in it. She looked a decade younger and happier. She was beautiful with her dark red hair and flashing green eyes.

He looked back down at the bed. It was the same face, but too thin now, and scarred by grief. He wanted to wipe away her tears but couldn't without waking her. He wanted to take away the pain but couldn't, because he didn't know how.

He was no good with people. He'd realised that a long time ago. Normally he didn't care, but this girl . . .

He caught the direction of his thoughts and angrily stopped them dead. This girl was nothing to him. Less than nothing. A lost cause foisted on him by his sister. A potential time bomb ticking away in his home. If he had any sense, he'd get rid of her before the explosion.

He looked down at her again and her eyes flickered open, as if she'd sensed his presence in her sleep. She stared at him unseeingly for a moment. She didn't seem to recognise him. He realised she was still in her past, still caught in the dark despair of that time.

'It's all right,' he spoke softly, his hand reaching out to brush the damp hair from her brow. 'I realised I'd upset you. I was worried,' he went on to explain, before she became afraid.

Clare, however, felt no fear. Her dreams had been much worse than reality. She was glad to be awake. His hand continued to stroke her face and she drew comfort from it. She stared back at him with the trust of a child.

She suddenly looked young, like the girl in the photograph. She was quite beautiful. The fact of it struck Fen Marchand hard. He knew he should go—had to go—then.

But he stayed.

There were no words between them.

He touched his lips to her forehead and Clare felt their warmth on her skin. Acutely aware of her loneliness, she suddenly didn't want to be alone any more. She shut her eyes and, in doing so, shut her mind to reality.

His lips moved, seeking hers, and she turned her head, but not away. Her mouth met his, and they kissed like lovers, long and hard and intimately, wanting more.

He lay down on the bed beside her, and drew her to him, his hands moving over her body. She felt his need and her own, and answered it. She pressed against him, and his hands became urgent, pushing up the jersey and vest she wore, stripping them off her, then removing his own shirt.

They made love in a hurry, as if they both knew they had only moments before sanity returned. He cupped her breasts in his large hands and sucked at each swollen nipple, and she moaned aloud. She arched to him, and he lifted his head to kiss her mouth again, while his hands pushed down her skirt and tights. He touched her, and found her warm and ready for him, her breathing betraying her own need for this hurried, frantic coupling.

He entered her, still half dressed. She felt a moment's pain and cried out, but it was followed by such pleasure that she held him to her. It was as if she'd been dead, and now she was alive, wonderfully, gloriously alive. He thrust into her, over and over, and she lifted to him, with the same desperate need. They came together, fast and hard.

It wasn't love, just sex. Neither pretended otherwise. They lay together afterwards, catching their breath, gathering their defences.

She pulled the bedclothes round her and he sat up, fastening his trousers. 'I shouldn't have,' was all he said.

He didn't even look at her. Perhaps he couldn't. Perhaps he was too ashamed of wanting, needing her.

She was ashamed, too. She had traded her pride for a moment's pleasure. Had it been worth it?

No, her mind cried as Fen Marchand rose from her bed and left without another word.

But her body cried out something different, as it relived every touch of his.

And her heart whispered something different still, only its voice was so tiny she could almost ignore it.

CHAPTER NINE

IT WAS her job so Clare made herself get up and prepare breakfast the next morning, all the time dreading their meeting.

He came down with Miles. She expected him to ignore her. She planned to ignore him.

Instead he went right to where she stood at the kitchen sink and asked, 'Are you all right?'

'Yes,' she snapped without looking at him.

She felt his eyes on her. He was assessing the damage. She looked as if she had barely slept. It wasn't surprising. She *had* barely slept.

'We have to talk,' he said in an undertone, before joining Miles at the table.

But Clare had no wish to talk. She served their breakfast with the indifference of a robot, then excused herself. She went upstairs again, and started packing her case.

He arrived as she was emptying her bookshelf. 'What are you doing, Clare?' he asked very calmly.

'What do you think?' she threw back at him.

'You can't leave.' It was a statement, not a plea.

'I can't stay,' she countered, and shot him an angry glance.

He stood in the doorway, respecting the sanctity of her room.

It was a pity he hadn't done so last night, Clare thought bitterly.

He looked quite composed, resolved. He obviously had no problems with what had happened. After all, what was she to him? Nothing.

'What do you want me to say?' His tone was so damn reasonable. 'That I won't touch you again? Is that really what you want?'

No, said her heart, but she hissed at him, 'Yes, that's what I want.'

She waited for him to call her a liar, but he didn't. It was almost humiliating. He just shrugged. 'Fair enough. You have my word. I'll leave you alone, if you stay.'

'I can't stay,' she repeated, struggling to match his cool manner.

'You have to, for Miles's sake,' he pointed out. 'From next week, I won't be able to collect him from school. A taxi can bring him home, but someone will have to be here for him. You agreed, remember?'

'Things have changed. *You* changed them,' she accused.

'Just me, was it?' His eyes rested on her face, then slid to the bed where they had made love.

Her face suffused with colour at the memory. He was right, damn him. She had been willing, more than willing.

'Still,' he continued ruthlessly, 'if you won't fulfil your obligations, I'll just have to tell Miles. He won't like it, but I have no choice.'

'What do you mean?'

'I'll have to put him into boarding-school after all.'

'That's blackmail!' she accused angrily. 'You can't expect me to stick around here until Miles is old enough to look after himself!'

'Perhaps not,' he agreed, his voice hardening, 'but I can expect you to honour your contract, requiring a month's notice. It'll give me a chance to find a new housekeeper.'

'A month?' Clare's tone made it sound like a prison sentence, and she knew all about those. But she weakened when she thought about Miles. He was just beginning to settle at Thomas Arnold's. 'Until half-term,' she calculated.

'That's three weeks,' he pointed out, 'but, yes, all right. Lou wants him to spend the holiday with her, so I won't need you then,' he dismissed.

He didn't need her full stop, and jealousy prompted Clare to scowl and retort, 'You could always go and stay with Professor Millar.'

'I never thought of that,' he countered, 'but it's an idea. Thanks.'

Thanks? Clare almost screamed back at him, and had to stop herself from throwing the book she was holding.

He knew. He looked from her to the novel in her hand, and he smiled. He actually smiled.

What game was he playing? Clare asked herself the question many times over the next few weeks. He was such a curious mixture of things to her.

For the first week, he behaved as if nothing had happened. He was polite in the face of her rudeness, friendly in the face of her hostility.

In the second week he started interviewing housekeepers, coming home from college to do so; he hadn't told Miles that she was leaving and had insisted she didn't. He would tell his son when he thought the time was right.

Clare didn't mind. She felt Miles would be ready to accept her departure by half-term. She didn't mind him interviewing for a new housekeeper, either. Obviously he had to find her replacement. It was his insistence on her sitting in on the interviews that galled her. Worse, he asked her opinion on each candidate.

She didn't know what he expected her to say. As far as she was concerned, none was good enough. Yes, to clean the house, but no, not to look after Miles. He needed someone special.

Mostly she shrugged rather than be specific, or agreed if he pointed out a fault, or simply refused to take part in his little charade.

She thought he was twisting the knife, and was tempted to repay him in some way. She got her chance on the fourth interview.

The candidate, a pleasant if rather untidy woman in her late thirties, asked her point-blank, 'Why are you leaving, may I ask?'

Fen had slipped out of the room for a moment, but he reappeared in time to catch the woman's question.

To Clare's surprise, he prompted, 'Feel free to answer, Miss Anderson. Be honest.'

'All right,' Clare gritted out, 'you want to know why I'm leaving? I'm leaving because ... because ...' She wanted to say it, to land him in it, but she couldn't seem to get the words out.

'Miss Anderson is obviously too shy to tell you,' Fen continued blandly, ignoring the look of horror on her face, 'but the truth is, I have fallen in love with her. This has caused her some embarrassment and, unable to return my feelings, she has decided to quit my employ.'

Clare's jaw dropped open. She couldn't believe what he'd just said. The lying toad!

The candidate's eyes widened as she looked from one to the other, questioning the truth of what she'd just been told. Then she tittered a little nervously, thinking it might be a joke. But, at Fen Marchand's deadpan expression, she decided it wasn't.

'How—um—awkward,' she finally concluded, her eyes sliding back to Clare.

Clare saw incredulity on the woman's face but it wasn't directed towards Fen. It was at her, questioning how she could possibly not return the feelings of this handsome, charming man.

Clare sat silently seething, waiting to explode the moment the woman was gone. She confronted him in the hall once they were alone.

'Is that your idea of a joke? Because if it is——' She searched for a suitable threat but found none. She couldn't threaten to leave. She was already leaving.

'What if it isn't?' he countered, his mouth a straight line.

He appeared serious but Clare wasn't a fool. How could he be in love with her? University dons didn't fall in love with household servants, especially ones with prison records.

'Oh, go to hell!' she muttered, not particularly under her breath, and walked away.

He stopped conducting interviews after that. She assumed he must have hired one of the women without her recommendation.

He continued to be pleasant despite her hostility. Sometimes, when she was downright rude, he would make some infuriating remark; for instance one day he said to her, 'You really are going to have to work on that attitude in a new post.'

When she didn't rise to the bait he asked her point-blank if she'd found another job yet. She told him it was none of his business. Not a very wise thing to say, as he responded, 'In that case, should I assume you don't want a reference?' Her face fell, realising her mistake, but he didn't leave her to sweat. 'Don't worry, you're the hardest-working housekeeper I've ever had. If anyone asks, that's what I'll say,' he promised in unequivocal tones.

'Thanks,' Clare said quietly, grateful that Fen was so fair-minded. But she didn't return his smile. She had to remain cold or...

Or what? she asked herself, already knowing the answer. She would weaken. She would forget the pain of love and remember just the loving. She knew he couldn't love her, but she knew she could all too easily love him.

It all changed in her final week. One morning she saw him at breakfast, and he was that infuriating mixture of pleasantness and irony. When he returned for dinner, he was like a different person. Not cold or indifferent—that would have been bearable. It was the way he talked to her, cruelly contemptuous. It was the way he looked at her, as if he could see inside her head, and didn't like what he saw.

She wanted to ask him what was wrong. What had she done? But he was so unapproachable, it proved impossible. She just began to count down to Saturday, her day of departure.

She had made no firm plans. Louise was coming to collect Miles and take him back to London. She had invited Clare to come along for the holiday week, but Clare had refused. It was clear from the telephone conversation that Lou had no idea Clare was leaving, and Clare decided it was up to Fen to do the explaining. If she decided to return to the capital, she would make her own way.

Initially she would stay in a bed and breakfast in Oxford for a few days. Her driving test was booked for the Tuesday and she would be a fool to miss the chance of having a licence that might improve her job prospects.

Fen had not cancelled her lessons, but, when he arrived home at lunchtime on the Friday, he was less than pleased to find her on the point of leaving with Paul Dyson.

'I came home so we could talk,' he announced as they met on the doorstep.

'Talk?' Clare frowned. 'About what?'

'What do you think?' he almost growled back. 'About us. About what we're doing——'

'I know what *I'm* doing,' Clare resorted to flippancy, 'I'm going for a driving lesson... So if you would excuse me...'

He was blocking her path. She went to move round him and he gripped her arm. He seemed oblivious of Paul Dyson, standing by his car, watching.

'Paul's waiting,' she said, trying and failing to twist from his grip.

'Are you all right, Clare?' the instructor called out to her.

'*Paul*? *Clare*?' Fen Marchand echoed the first names with a sneer. 'So you have got friendly... Well, *are* you all right, Clare? Tell the man!'

No, she wasn't all right. How could she be all right, when he looked at her as if he hated her? She looked back at him, questioning what she'd done to make him feel that way.

He didn't answer, although he could read the confusion on her face. Instead he dropped his hand away, and instructed, 'Go on. I'll see you before I go and collect Miles from school.'

He went inside and she was left to join Paul Dyson. She fended off his curiosity about the scene he'd witnessed and tried her best to concentrate on the lesson. It was over all too soon, and for the first time she took up Dyson's offer of a drink in the local pub at the crossroads. She listened to his arrogant chat-up routine for another hour, before she calculated that Fen would have left to fetch Miles, then she insisted that Dyson take her home. She didn't tell him of her imminent departure from Woodside Hall but simply arranged a time to meet him in Oxford on the day of her test.

Fen's car was gone on her return and she let herself into the house. She went upstairs to pack, but heard the doorbell, and came down again.

A smartly dressed young woman stood on the doorstep. Recognition was not immediate for Clare.

Nor was it for the other woman, although she said tentatively, 'Clare... Clare Anderson?'

Clare nodded slowly, and looked past the coiffured blonde hair and ultra-chic suit to identify her caller. She felt shock and dismay.

'It's me—Sarah,' the woman introduced herself although it was no longer necessary.

'Yes, I know.' Clare stared at Johnny's sister without welcome.

'I have to talk to you. May I come in?' She looked past Clare into the hall.

But Clare barred her way. She couldn't let her in. Any moment Fen might return with Miles and she didn't want her old life meeting her new.

'I can't... My boss will be home soon.'

Sarah frowned, but accepted that there might be a problem. 'Later, then. Could we meet somewhere?'

'I don't know.' Clare couldn't believe they had anything to say. Sarah might be the one Holstead who'd never treated her badly, but she'd hardly been a friend, either.

'I have to see you,' Sarah urged. 'It's important.'

'Tomorrow, in Oxford, I could——' Clare began to suggest.

'I'm sorry, it has to be today,' Sarah insisted. 'I go away on holiday tomorrow with the children. I have three now.'

'Oh.' Clare remembered she'd had a toddler and was pregnant with another at the time of the trial. It seemed that life had moved on for everybody else but her. 'Your parents—do they know you're here?'

The other woman shook her head. 'No, Father's dead. He died last month. That's partly why I need to see you.'

Clare frowned. She didn't see what Lord Abbotsford's death would have to do with her. She felt no sympathy so didn't express any. She didn't really want any further contact with Johnny's family, and was about to say so, when Fen's car appeared on the drive.

'You have to go,' she urged Sarah.

'All right,' the other woman nodded, 'but not before you give me a time and place.'

'After dinner... nine?' Clare thought fast. 'It's the earliest I can manage. And it'll have to be the pub. It's about quarter of a mile down the road, at the Oxford crossroads.'

'What's it called?'

'The Old Corn Mill.'

'I'll find it,' Sarah assured her, offering Clare a quick smile as she switched to saying, 'I feel such a fool getting lost. Thanks for your help. Good afternoon.'

She turned on her heel and gave a brief nod to Fen before walking back to her car—a stylish Mercedes.

'Who was that?' Fen eyed the departing car with suspicion.

Clare shrugged. 'Just a passer-by. She's trying to find the Old Corn Mill.'

It wasn't so far from the truth and he accepted it with a dismissive shrug, before saying, 'We still have to talk. I've promised to play chess with Miles before dinner, so it'll have to be after.'

'I can't.' Clare was relieved that she had an excuse. 'I'm going out.'

'Out?' He looked first surprised, then disbelieving. 'Out where?'

'On a date.' She said the first thing that came into her head.

His disbelief changed to anger as he coldly asserted, 'Dyson.'

It wasn't a question, but a statement. It seemed easier not to dispute it.

He took her silence as assent, and, with a look of contempt, walked past her inside.

At dinner she might have been invisible. He didn't talk to her. He didn't even look at her. She had ceased to exist.

It made her angry. She didn't sneak out at quarter to nine. No, she walked out in full view, head high.

Lady Sarah was already waiting at the pub. She was with her husband—a grey-haired man of about forty. He made himself scarce, first fetching the drinks, then going to sit at the bar.

Clare sat patiently while Sarah talked nervously, chattering on about her children and her husband, and their lives. It was some time before she got round to asking Clare about her own life.

Clare realised eventually why they were there. Sarah felt guilty. Guilty that she had said nothing at her trial. She had known of her brother's drug habit. She had known Peter was Johnny's child. She had worked out why Clare had stolen the horse. Yet she had sat with her parents in the courtroom and maintained the family silence.

Clare allowed Sarah to talk. Her attention was on the present, not the past. She wondered what Fen was doing—drinking to celebrate her departure?

She was only half listening when Sarah let slip how she'd found her. Till then, Clare had assumed it had been through the prison and hostel.

'A woman called you for a reference?' Clare echoed. 'What woman?'

'She didn't give her name,' Sarah relayed. 'She just said she was a friend of Professor Marchand's and that you were working as his housekeeper and he wanted to know how trustworthy you were. I tried to be as evasive as possible but she already seemed to know most of it— about you helping to steal Blue Dancer and the drug charge concerning Johnny... I did try and give her the true picture.'

'Do you know the true picture?' Clare's tone was sceptical.

'I think so,' Sarah replied quietly. 'I think you stole Dancer for money to help your son. I don't believe you knowingly supplied Johnny with drugs, or, if you did, he gave you no choice... What I don't understand is why you never explained any of this at your trial.'

Clare shrugged. She hadn't cared at the time. She countered, 'Why didn't you?'

Sarah had the grace to look ashamed. 'Fear of Daddy, I suppose. He and Mummy couldn't accept that they and not you had caused Johnny to ruin his life... Anyway, I want to make it up to you now.'

Clare didn't understand until the other woman went into her handbag and placed the cheque in front of her.

Thirty thousand pounds. The amount she had received as her cut from Blue Dancer. Was it a coincidence or did Sarah imagine it was payment for the years she'd spent in prison?

She picked up the cheque. She felt anger, but it was the cool kind. She ripped the cheque in two. She had no second thoughts.

'No, thanks,' she said simply, and, rising from her chair, made for the door.

Sarah followed. 'Clare, I'm sorry. I did that badly. I want you to have the money. It's what you deserve.'

Clare shook her head. The money was four years too late. She didn't need it now.

'Is it forgiveness you want?' Clare asked, her smile pitying. 'Then have it. I forgive you, free of charge.'

She slipped out of the door before Sarah could detain her further. She walked away, and, in doing so, left behind her past.

She walked down the country road, oblivious of the darkness and possible danger. Her mind was already racing ahead to what she might say to *Professor* Marchand.

It was his actions that were *unforgivable*. If he had wanted to know her crimes, he could have done his own investigating. He could have asked Lou or the prison authorities or even a private detective. To allow Ros Millar to do his dirty work for him was the lowest, most contemptible thing she had ever heard. And she knew he had, because why else had he been treating her like a leper all week?

He was waiting for her when she returned. She was on the second stair when he appeared from the living-room.

'Gone home to his wife, has he?' he sneered at her.

'What?' It was a moment before Clare recalled that she was meant to have been out with Dyson. 'I don't know.'

'And you don't care,' he read into her offhand tone.

She shrugged, then, seeing the dark temper lurking in his eyes, decided tonight was not the time for a fight. She continued on up the stairs.

She thought he'd let her go. She was wrong. He caught her up at the top step.

'Leave me alone,' she cried at him, and managed to shrug his hand off. He caught her again as she walked along the landing.

'We need to talk,' he growled out, and, when she would have twisted free, pushed her back against a wall.

'What about?' she threw back.

'About us,' he grated, his face almost white with anger.

'*Us*—there is no us.' There was pain beneath Clare's scorn. Why was he doing this to her?

He raised a hand to her throat, forcing her head up. His eyes searched her face for the truth. His body pressed against hers, and her breathing became shallow. His fingers spread from her neck to her cheek. Anger seemed to change to something else.

'Isn't there?' he taunted softly. 'Then why are you trembling?'

'I...I...' She licked her lips, a nervous gesture. He followed the movement with his eyes, then a finger, tracing the moist outline of her mouth. She felt desire curl in her stomach. She shook her head. 'Why are you doing this?' she said in a tone of appeal.

'I want you,' he replied with blunt simplicity.

Her anger returned. 'You've had me, remember?'

'I want you again and again,' he added, and, before she could stop him, covered her lips with his.

He kissed her hard. She tried to push him away. He caught her wrists and held them on either side of her head. He continued kissing her, forcing her to accept this inevitability, this elemental feeling for each other, until finally she opened her lips for him. He tasted her sweetness with the thrust of his tongue. She moaned aloud and tried to free one arm—whether to push him away or hold him she didn't know. But he kept her arms pinned where they were as his mouth slid from hers to kiss her neck, bite gently on the lobe of her ear, press on her temple where the pulse beat with fear and excitement.

'I don't——' She tried to tell him she didn't want him, but the words got lost, caught in her throat as his mouth covered hers once more.

He let her arms fall and put his own round her, gathering her close to him. She felt her heart twist with that sweet, dreadful pain, not of desire, but of love.

She loved him. She finally accepted it. She loved this man, and it was terrifying.

She tried to hold on to her pride, her sanity, but her head was spinning, her heart reeling. Still kissing her mouth, he led her along the corridor.

'No, it's wrong,' she heard herself breathe against his mouth as he pulled her into his room.

But he just urged, 'Don't talk,' and kept kissing her, as they reached his bed in the darkness.

She still wore her coat. He pushed it off her shoulders, down her arms, then fell with her on to the bed.

She knew she could stop him. She just had to say *no* and mean it. But she was weak. She wanted his love—or all he was able to give her.

He started kissing her again. She returned his kisses, sliding her arms round his neck to hold him to her. She felt his heart hammering against hers.

He broke off the kiss and she felt him move away from her, but it was only to switch on the light by the bed.

Clare would have preferred the darkness. A frown creased her forehead.

'I want you to know it's me.' He almost growled the words, and pulled her round to face him.

Clare's frown deepened. Why was he angry with her?

She would have turned from him but he reached out a hand and caught her chin. Their eyes met and held. The way he looked at her was a mixture of desire and disdain. It was crippling. She shut her eyes. She tried to find the strength to reject him, and might have found it, if he hadn't moved his hand to caress her cheek.

He traced the outline of her face with one long finger. 'You're beautiful,' he whispered.

Clare lifted her eyes once more to his in denial of what he was saying. He couldn't find her beautiful. She had lost her looks a long time ago.

But she couldn't deny that he wanted her. He looked at her with total desire. She felt the same in return.

Only nothing was so simple for her. It wasn't desire that would leave her hurting. It was the love that went along with it. She'd been on this road before and knew where it led.

Yet she lay there, letting him take her along. She lay there, while he slowly unbuttoned her blouse and drew it from her shoulders, down her arms. She lay there, trembling, while he unfastened and removed the bra she wore.

He looked at her breasts, small but well-shaped, with dark aureoles. Uncertain of her attraction, she crossed an arm over her chest.

'Don't.' His fingers gently encircled her wrist and drew her arm away. 'They're beautiful ... perfect ...'

His eyes caressed her skin, but he seemed in no hurry to touch her. Instead he unbuttoned his own shirt, and stripped it off.

She'd never seen him unclothed and she was surprised by his very maleness. His chest was broad and covered in dark blond hair, tapering to his waist.

He reached out an arm and drew her to him. Her breasts swelled, soft against the roughness of his hair-coarsened chest. He held her there for what seemed a timeless moment, her heart beating hard against his, and she could almost imagine they were lovers in every sense.

He pushed her back on the bed, and fastened his mouth to hers. They kissed as people did when love was new. They kissed as if they would never be able to get enough of each other. They threaded their fingers through one another's hair and held the other to them and kissed until they couldn't breathe.

Then he took his mouth away and trailed his lips down her body, tasting the slight sheen of sweat on her skin from the heat of his, touching the pulse leaping wildly at her neck, moving downwards slowly, too slowly, until she offered her breast to him and he took the swollen peak in his mouth. Gently, at first, he licked round the dark aureole, teasing, exciting, then, with a rough sensuality, he began to play and suck and bite on her soft, yielding flesh, so that she moaned with the wild pleasure of it. She dug her nails into his back, wanting him to stop, wanting him to go on, forgetting all else.

His hands moved to her hips and raised them to his. She felt the hardness of his body. She felt that confusing mixture of fear and excitement, but didn't stop him, as he drew the zip of her skirt down and pushed the garment from her hips.

He rose from the bed, leaving her naked except for a pair of briefs. She lay there, breathing hard. He watched her as he stripped off his trousers. His eyes told her he found her beautiful.

He lay down beside her again, murmuring, 'This time's for you,' and began to make slow, sensuous love to her, kissing her mouth, her breasts, touching, touching all of her, hand splaying out on the flat of her belly, downwards, slipping between the silk of skin and underwear, spreading, seeking, finding the already moist core of her being. And still he pleasured her, denying his own needs, as he made her ready—more than ready, as she arched beneath his touch.

He raised himself above her and for a moment was completely still. He waited until she opened her eyes, waited until she looked into his, and recognised him as her lover.

In that moment Clare saw love in his face, and reached up for him, joined with him, moved with him, gave and gave, cried out her passion as she accepted his, over and over, in a coupling so perfect they might have been lovers for a century. He called her name and she called his as he gave her his seed and she gave him her love.

It was both real and unreal. They lay in each other's arms, silent. Then, still silent, they loved again. Then slept.

She woke first. It was near dawn. The bedside light had been switched off, but the curtains were open. Soon autumn sunlight would fill the room and she would not be able to hide in its brightness.

She lay for a moment and looked at the head on the pillow next to her. Awake, he was handsome. In sleep, he was beautiful, hardness gone. She looked at him with all the love in her heart, then, killing such weakness, rose from the bed.

She was dressed before he woke. He did so suddenly, going from sleep to alertness in an instant.

'Where are you going?' he asked, although he probably understood well enough.

'To my room.' She prayed that he would just let her go.

She made for the door. It was at his side of the bed. He rose and blocked her exit before she could get round. He was still naked. She looked at him for a moment, then looked away.

It was stupid to be shy. She knew his body. She had touched it in the night, as he had touched hers. But it was day now and they were enemies again and his nakedness forced her to remember their intimacy.

She realised he meant to stop her leaving. She went into retreat, walking back towards the window which looked out on the courtyard. She stared down the drive while he pulled on his trousers.

'We must talk,' he said, coming to stand behind her, 'about where we go from here.'

Clare shook her head, refusing to listen. 'I'm leaving, remember?' she replied in a tone that was deliberately hard.

She was punished for it, as he grabbed her arm and spun her round. 'You're *leaving*? Just like that? Didn't last night mean anything to you?'

It had meant everything to her, but Clare doubted it had meant much to him. So why was he making everything so difficult?

'What do you want me to say? It was great, fantastic?' she jeered angrily. 'All right—it was great, fan——'

'You bitch!' he cut in harshly, adding in a low growl, 'I could kill you sometimes.'

He looked as if he meant it. She tried to wrest free, but he caught both her arms.

'Is it Dyson?' he went on wildly. 'Are you going to him?'

'*Dyson*?' Her tone told him how absurd he was being. 'Paul Dyson is my driving instructor, end of story. Anything else is in your imagination,' she stated with a steely ring of truth.

He accepted it, but still demanded, 'Then what do you want of me?' dragging her face close to his. 'What does it take? Money, marriage...what? Name it!'

'*Marriage*?' Clare repeated in absolute disbelief. 'You'd never marry *me*!'

'Why not?' His lips twisted in contempt.

Clare could hardly contain her temper. 'Don't be absurd! You know why not.'

'No, enlighten me,' he clipped back.

Clare stared at him, sure it must be some cruel joke. 'Professors at Oxford colleges don't marry servants, even when they don't have criminal records.'

'I don't give a damn about status,' he rapped back, 'and, as for your record, at least this time I'd know what I was getting.'

'Really! And what would you be getting?' She challenged him to say just what he thought of her.

He grimaced, before stating, 'I have been advised of your past history.'

'"Advised"?' she echoed his choice of words. 'God, you're so pompous at times! Why don't you just admit that Ros Millar did your dirty work for you? I bet she enjoyed relaying all the juicy bits.'

'I didn't *ask* Mrs Millar to investigate your background,' he declared emphatically. 'She did it for her own reasons.'

'But you listened, didn't you?' she accused, then her own jealousy surfaced as she added, 'Pillow talk, was it?'

'No, it was not,' he denied icily, 'nor could it have been. I have never slept with Ros Millar. The nights I didn't come home I spent at my college rooms, keeping away from you!' he explained tersely.

Clare believed him but her jealousy didn't subside. Ros Millar was so much more suitable. She was sophisticated, intellectual, respectable—everything Clare wasn't.

'Ros Millar is an irrelevance,' he dismissed. 'The point is I don't care about your past.'

'Yes, you do,' Clare countered. 'You've treated me like a social leper since you heard what I really was inside for.'

'All right, I care,' he admitted heavily, 'but I can live with it—if you'll live with me.'

Clare heard his words, if not the meaning behind them as she challenged, 'For how long? A week, a month, a year? Till you tire of me. And then what? Do I get pensioned off like a faithful servant?' She sneered at what she really saw as his plan. Not a proposal so much as a proposition. 'Well, I don't get used like that, not twice,' she finished bitterly.

'Is that what happened with you and John Holstead?' he asked point-blank. 'Did he pay you off when you were having his baby?'

'Does it matter?' Clare didn't want to go into the past.

But he pursued, 'Yes, it matters! Did he?'

Clare shook her head. 'I didn't tell him. He was already on to pastures new—a suitably rich, suitably aristocratic fiancée. My mother helped me out—or, at least, gave me enough for a private abortion. I used it to start a new life.'

'But you went back,' he persisted with a bitter edge. 'Couldn't you keep away from him?'

'Johnny?' She shook her head and turned to look out of the window once more as she relayed, 'I went back for my mother. She was dying of cancer. I had no interest in any of the Holsteads.'

'Just their money,' he suggested bluntly.

She shrugged, then agreed, 'Yes, their money.'

'So you stole a horse from their stables,' he recounted the details Ros Millar had given him.

It was the truth, and Clare didn't see the point in qualifying it. Nodding, she continued to stare out on the courtyard.

He stood beside her, his eyes fixed on her profile as he added, 'And, having then sold it, you supplied heroin to Johnny Holstead, on which he overdosed.'

'Something like that.' Clare was too proud to explain herself.

She waited for his derision. She didn't expect anything else, certainly not a response of, 'I don't believe you.'

She turned her head and met his steady gaze. She saw neither anger nor puzzlement, just exasperation.

'What do you mean?' she demanded.

'What I said,' he clipped back. 'Why don't you tell me the truth?'

He was giving her a chance. She could explain the way it had really been. But was there any point?

'What difference would it make?' she sighed. 'I could
tell you now why I stole the horse. I could tell you I
never knowingly gave Johnny drugs. But what does it
change?' she added, her voice breaking a little.

She looked up at him, green eyes appealing for him
to let it go—to let *her* go. But his eyes caught and held
hers, and something did change. They forgot for a
moment that they were fighting, and remembered last
night when they had been lovers.

'You're right,' he agreed quietly; 'it changes nothing.
I want you no matter what.'

He lifted a hand to touch her cheek. She backed away
and came hard up against a wall.

'Don't...' she appealed.

He ignored her. 'And you want me. The rest is irrelevant. You have to stay.'

'I can't stay,' she cried at him. 'I have to go now. If
I don't——' She broke off before she could admit her
weakness.

But he knew. 'Why does it scare you so much? Do
you think I'd treat you like Johnny Holstead?'

She shook her head. They were very different men.
Johnny hadn't even been a man, just a weak, selfish
boy. She knew now she'd never really loved him.

But she did love Fen; only loving him didn't make her
blind to the impossibilities. Even if he could live with
her past, she was light-years away from his ideal partner.

'No, but you *would* tire of me.' She spoke her thoughts
aloud. 'It's inevitable. You need someone well-read and
witty and intellectual, someone like——'

'Ros Millar,' he supplied for her. 'Well, I don't want
Ros Millar. I want you. And this new-found humility
doesn't suit you... Don't you think I know how bright
you are?' he asked exasperatedly.

Clare looked at him in surprise. She'd always assumed that he dismissed her intelligence because of her
lack of college education.

Finding herself weakening, wanting to stay, Clare went on the attack. 'You say you want me. But you don't! You just want to sleep with me!' she accused bluntly.

'Actually, no.' A hint of a smile played on his lips. 'I want to do far more interesting things than *sleep*. However,' he continued as she visibly stiffened, 'I'll settle for less. Stay on as housekeeper or guest or whatever you choose, and give us time to work on our relationship. If you do, I'll promise to keep away from you—and this time I'll do it, even if it kills me.'

Clare stared at him in disbelief. It was almost as if he was suggesting a courtship, but surely he knew he didn't have to court her. She had no resistance to him. Only pride had kept her out of his bed till now.

'Is it Miles?' she asked suspiciously. 'Because if it is, and you haven't been able to find another housekeeper, then say so. You don't have to pretend——'

'*Pretend*?' he almost exploded at her. 'Do you think I was pretending last night? Were you?' He grasped her arms once more.

She saw the way out. She just had to lie, tell him she had been pretending.

'I...' She tried, but hesitated too long.

He pulled her to him, and, before she could stop him, kissed her hard on the mouth. He stole her breath, her will, her heart. Her body swayed against his like a willow in a storm. It was he who broke off, pushing her back against the wall.

'Tell me you don't feel anything!' he demanded.

'You said it was just sex,' she accused him.

'Well, what did you expect me to say?' He matched her anger. 'Do you think it's easy—loving someone who doesn't give a damn about you?'

Clare shook her head, refusing to be taken in. 'You don't love me!' she cried back at him.

'You think I want to!' he almost snarled at her.

'You *can't* love me.' It seemed an impossible dream to Clare. 'Not if you still believe I'm a thief and a drug dealer.'

'I don't know what I believe,' he admitted hoarsely. 'My heart—and my head, for that matter—doesn't accept you are either of those things. Yet the facts suggest otherwise. If you'd just trust me with the truth——' he urged, his hands tightening on her arms.

Again, he was giving her a chance, but Clare was frightened of taking it.

'You'll just think it's a sob story,' she said tightly, and would have walked past him if he hadn't stopped her. Resigned, she added, 'OK, I'll tell you...'

And she did. She told the whole story in concise, un-emotional terms. He didn't interrupt. It took no more than five minutes to relay her brief relationship with Johnny Holstead, the baby that had resulted, her child's illness, her need for money.

He interrupted at that point. 'Did you know you were stealing the horse with Holstead?'

'Johnny told me he had his father's permission,' she recalled, 'but yes, I suppose I knew otherwise. I just didn't care.'

He nodded and muttered, 'Fair enough... And the drugs?'

She explained briefly how she'd acted as Johnny's messenger and the outcome.

'But you didn't realize the package contained drugs?' he quizzed again.

She shook her head. 'I had no idea, but I couldn't prove it.'

She waited for him to say something—either express belief or disbelief. He was silent but she sensed his anger.

'You think it's rubbish,' she accused, and, jerking free, managed to walk towards the door.

He caught her up and pulled her round. 'On the con-trary. Knowing you, it sounds all too plausible. I just can't believe you were gaoled in those circumstances.'

His anger wasn't directed at her but at the unfairness of it all. 'Didn't the Holsteads come forward? They must have known their son was responsible.'

Clare sighed. 'It was easier for them to keep Johnny as the victim. That's what his sister says, anyway.'

'You've been in touch with her?' he asked sharply.

'Only once. Last night, as a matter of fact,' she stated pointedly, refuting any liaison with Paul Dyson. 'I agreed to meet her in the pub.'

'The woman in the afternoon who was meant to be lost,' he concluded.

'Yes, that was Sarah.'

'Ros Millar's enquiries prompted her visit?'

Clare nodded.

'What did she want?' he added.

'Nothing much,' Clare shrugged, before admitting carelessly, 'She just offered me some money—thirty thousand pounds, actually.'

'Thirty-thousand pounds?' He looked impressed by the amount. 'That's some conscience money.'

'Yes, I suppose it is,' Clare agreed, then added flatly, 'I didn't take it.'

'You should have,' he told her, a suggestion of a smile in his voice. 'Then you could have accused me of marrying you for your money.'

'You won't marry me,' she said, only now with less certainty. 'You can't. Even if you believe me——'

'I do,' he cut in.

'And even if you love me——'

'I do,' he cut in again.

'And even if I loved you——'

'Do you?' he cut in a third time.

Clare looked cross rather than loving. 'That's beside the point.'

'Really?' He slanted his head to one side and watched as her face went a betraying pink. 'I'd say it was exactly the point. I love you. And call me conceited but I think you may just love me. So what stands in our way?

Nothing, other than *your* pride,' he answered his own question.

Quite unfairly, Clare thought as she challenged, 'My pride?'

'Quite,' he said, as if agreeing. 'You assume the rest of the world won't consider a housekeeper a suitable partner for an Oxford don. But your pride tells you that, if anything, you're too good for me... Ergo you'd make us both miserable, just so no one could say, Hasn't she done well for herself?'

'That's ridiculous!' Clare almost exploded rather than admit his astuteness.

'Yes, isn't it?' he agreed. 'So why not just marry me and damn the rest of the world?'

'I...you're...' She searched futilely for a response, but before she could find one they were interrupted.

With a brief knock, Miles suddenly appeared at the door. He looked from a dishevelled Clare to a half-dressed Fen, worked things out for himself, and with a grinning, 'Oops,' backed out of the door.

'Caught in the act,' Fen concluded with a wry smile not dissimilar to his son's. 'Well, that does it. You'll have to marry me now.'

'You could go after him and explain,' Clare suggested, but without much urgency, as he slipped his arms round her waist and drew her to him.

'Too complicated,' he murmured before lowering his mouth to hers and kissing her until they were both breathless. 'Much easier just to face the music.'

'The music?' Clare felt all sanity and reason slipping away, but didn't seem to mind.

'Da-dum-d-da, da-dum-d-da,' he began to sing rather badly, and she laughed aloud.

She hadn't laughed for five years. She hadn't snug. She hadn't danced. She had just survived.

Now she stood on the edge of a new life, and it was both magnificent and terrifying. It was a jump into the unknown and she was scared rigid.

She stood there, trembling. She looked at him with all the doubt and the fear of being hurt that had made her head rule her heart for so long and she refused to jump. She backed away, but he took her hand, and jumped with her.

It was an unconventional courtship. Everybody said so. It led to a hasty marriage. Suspiciously hasty, everybody said, too. But, with time, the strength of their love became evident, encompassing first Miles, then the baby that came in their second year. And after that everybody said what a perfectly matched couple they were.

None of it mattered to Clare or Fen. They lived for each other, and ignored the rest of the world. They argued and fought and made up and fell out again, but that didn't matter either.

For their love was strong and confident and real and imperfect—just as they were.

As a Privileged Woman,
you'll be entitled to all
these Free Benefits.
And Free Gifts, too.

To thank you for buying our books, we've designed an exclusive FREE program called *PAGES & PRIVILEGES™*. You can enroll with just one Proof of Purchase, and get the kind of luxuries that, until now, you could only read about.

BIG HOTEL DISCOUNTS

A privileged woman stays in the finest hotels. And so can you—at up to 60% off! Imagine standing in a hotel check-in line and watching as the guest in front of you pays $150 for the same room that's only costing you $60. Your *Pages & Privileges* discounts are good at Sheraton, Marriott, Best Western, Hyatt and thousands of other fine hotels all over the U.S., Canada and Europe.

FREE DISCOUNT TRAVEL SERVICE

A privileged woman is always jetting to romantic places. When <u>you</u> fly, just make one phone call for the lowest published airfare at time of booking—<u>or double the difference back!</u> PLUS— you'll get a $25 voucher to use the first time you book a flight AND <u>5% cash back on every ticket you buy thereafter through the travel service!</u>

MILLION DOLLAR SWEEPSTAKES (III)

𝓕REE GIFTS!

A privileged woman is always getting wonderful gifts.
Luxuriate in rich fragrances that will stir your senses (and his). This gift-boxed assortment of fine perfumes includes three popular scents, each in a beautiful designer bottle. _Truly Lace_...This luxurious fragrance unveils your sensuous side. _L'Effleur_...discover the romance of the Victorian era with this soft floral. _Muguet des bois_...a single note floral of singular beauty.

𝓕REE INSIDER TIPS LETTER

A privileged woman is always informed. And you'll be, too, with our free letter full of fascinating information and sneak previews of upcoming books.

𝓜ORE GREAT GIFTS & BENEFITS TO COME

A privileged woman always has a lot to look forward to. And so will you. You get all these wonderful FREE gifts and benefits now with only one purchase...and there are no additional purchases required. However, each additional retail purchase of Harlequin and Silhouette books brings you a step closer to even more great FREE benefits like half-price movie tickets... and even more FREE gifts.

L'Effleur...This basketful of romance lets you discover L'Effleur from head to toe, heart to home.

Truly Lace...
A basket spun with the sensuous luxuries of Truly Lace, including Dusting Powder in a reusable satin and lace covered box.

Complete the Enrollment Form in the front of this book and mail it with this Proof of Purchase.

PROOF OF PURCHASE
Offer expires October 31, 1996

HP-PP3